IN THE NORTH

IN THE NORTH
Being the First Adventure of Burton the Red

by

Sandro Dariosto

per sempre Anita Edizione
Ferrara Seattle
2014

This is a work of fiction. Names, characters, places, and
incidents are either the work of the author's imagination or are
used fictitiously.

Printed in the United States of America

per sempre Anita Edizione
via delle Scienze 17 Ferrara

10 9 8 7 6 5 4 3 2 1

Il Rosso in the North,
or
How Jack Burton Earned His Name

To the happy few

Ho un cuore che troppo senti.
--Francesco Anzani

"Butto Sam" was blazoned across the side of the cart in red carnival letters a foot tall, with a yellow as a daffodil trim. "Native Upland Gorilla from the African Islands of Darkest Zambutti far off the Cape of Lost Hope," read the print beneath his mighty name.

The gorilla inside that cage came here from the mountainous island of Zambutti, the circus barker had claimed. It was two hundred miles off the coast of South Africa, hauled across the big waters in a crate without bars or windows, with only narrow vents, to sit in the sweltering mid-western American humidity hidden inside a wheeled cart towed behind a big red Buick convertible, to the sound of hurdy-gurdy music and carnival pitches.

What a sweatbox that cart was. How was he fed inside there? I wondered. Did he ever see the light of day? Or the moon and the stars at night?

We understood his suffering, but it only intensified the mystery of that darkness, and of the black beast helpless and caged inside it. I could taste danger at the back of my throat, and for me it was intoxicating.

Our long quest to find Jack Burton began with a simple desire to see what lay down inside the black, barred darkness of a gorilla's cage.

But I was too short, and the little barred window above the t's in Butto Sam's name was too high. There would be no peaking in, not at this black mystery "from the African Islands," not for free anyway. Butto Sam was a paying attraction. So I stood there without even any change in my pocket, gazing up at those bars, hungry for a look.

My little brother stood beside me in short pants, with his back to the cage, staring big eyed at the white circus horses and the one lone elephant chained to the grounds of the schoolyard, all of them grazing together peacefully, like Iowa livestock fattening in the fields. Our little brown dog George sat beside me, with the same glaze of wonderment in his eyes as my kid brother's. "Butto Sam," I whispered, reading the side of the cart.

"Hey, Robbie, " I said. "You want a look at Butto Sam?"

"At who?" Robbie said, and turned the shining bifocals he wore at me.

You see, I realized that there was no way I could climb up high enough to see down through the barred window of that cage. But Robbie could, by golly. If I could boost him up high enough, he could lean on the walls of that cart and maybe he could peer through the thick flat bars and see down into the dark, to the beast below.

"The Upland Gorilla," I barked at him. Didn't he know who Butto Sam was?

2

Robbie looked up at the high window, and said, "I don't know," sounding more than a little suspicious of what I might be up to.

And I suppose he should have been, since this was hardly the first time I'd come up with an idea that had me safe on the ground while he hung his little behind out over the vast ravine of danger, waving like a flag in the summer breeze. George turned and looked up at me. His scraggly curled tail wagged once, I guess just at the excitement in my voice.

Looming tall above Butto Sam's cart stood our three-storey schoolhouse. High as the clouds and a hundred years old and filled with dust in the empty unused floors, its yellow sandstone walls standing there like they came from the far away desert and the distant beyond, and they framed that gorilla's name in everything that home and school wasn't. Butto Sam, the hidden beast beyond the Cape of All Lost Hopes.

"C'mon, Robbie," I hissed. "I'll boost you up there, and then you tell me what he looks like."

"Who?" my little brother said again.

"What? Are you scared, or something?" I said, my voice rising to a squeak I didn't intend. "Butto Sam!" I pointed at the big red letters on the cart, and at the little window too, I guess. "That's who!" I yelled.

There was no way for Robbie to back down now. "Okay," he said tentatively. He put both his little palms against the wall of Butto Sam's cart, and with my help, as I held his waist, he stepped up on my bended knees.

"Ready?" I said through my clamped teeth.

"Yeah," Robbie sounded a little unsure.

"I'm gonna lift your left foot up on my shoulder," I said.

As I boosted that foot up onto my shoulder, he walked his palms slowly up the wall of that cart, with a teetering

3

thump, thump, thump. Then, we got his other foot up onto my shoulder, and I grunted up at him, "Stand up!" It took another breath, but I managed to add, "Straight!"

I clung to the tire of the cart with both hands to steady myself, hoping to keep my knees from buckling under my little brother's weight. Straining my eyes to see up between his legs, I pulled myself up until I was standing, and Robbie's hands pounded on the walls of the cart some more as he walked them upwards. In a moment or so, we were straight up and teetering in the breeze. We couldn't last that way for long. George was now wending his way around my ankles, his wagging tail lapping at my shins.

"Can you see him?" I blurted out. All I could see was the round bulge of Robbie's tummy under his t-shirt. The strain of trying to speak made me wobble a bit, and for a moment I thought my knees might give out. That sent a tremor up into Robbie's knees, and we nearly crumpled. But I pulled myself steady again on that cart tire, and I heard Robbie's palms slapping on the walls of the cart to get his balance back again.

Then, awakening at the noise, the ape stirred in his cage. I heard a low, soft growl like a grumble from inside, in answer to my grunts and Robbie's slapping palms on the cart. George, standing between my legs, started to growl back at the stirrings of Butto Sam, the Upland Gorilla.

"Can you see him?" I grunted again, because I knew we couldn't last like this for long, a two-tiered tower of wobbly legs and weakening knees. Emboldened by my grunts, George began to growl louder and end each growl with a sharp bark.

Robbie shoved his face up by the bars, and he nearly laid his bifocals against the flat iron. "It's dark in there," he said. "I can't see nothing."

"Look harder," I moaned out now, desperate for him to see something.

"It's too dark, " he said.

But then a pair of black eyes appeared behind the bars. They gazed directly out at Robbie, just inches from his bifocals. I know because Robbie said, "Geez-us!" And then pushed himself back, away from the window.

That sent me wobbling, flat-footed, in some kind of locked to the ground dance trying to keep him up on my shoulders. "Aaah," Robbie wheezed, yet somehow we stayed up and the two of us steadied our shaky tower.

"What d'ya see? " I said.

George growled and then barked fiercely between my legs.

"He's looking right at me," Robbie said, his voice quavering a little. But now my little brother was not moving.

"Whoa!" I said. I strained my head up to look past Robbie, to see what he was seeing. But all I could find between Robbie's outstretched arms were the flat iron bands of the window bars.

"He's looking right at me," Robbie repeated, but sounding calmer.

Oh, I hungered then to see what my little brother saw, standing on my shoulders, gazing deep into those brown black eyes of wildness, seeing down into the wells of light shining up from out of that darkness, from the beast who dwelled on the islands of the African south, from far below the Equator, south past all the horns of Africa, south and south toward the pole on the horizon, staring out at me. In my mind I could see the twinkle of true danger in the untamed eyes of Butto Sam. But I wasn't seeing anything.

All I could really see was inside of Robbie's striped t-shirt, the dimple of his belly button over my head, and above that, if I twisted back my neck until I couldn't breathe, the flat iron bars of Butto Sam's cage.

But then, slowly, four fat, round fingers emerged from the darkness inside the window, followed gradually by a black thick thumb on the other side of the bar. As slowly as a calm lion pacing in its pen, the fingers of Butto Sam wrapped carefully around one of those flat iron bars, and gently held it tight. Underneath that slow, deliberate pace you could sense the pent up power of the great ape.

"Oh, geez," Robbie whispered.

That hand was big enough even I could see those black fingers with their graying knuckles. They were only inches from Robbie's bifocals, but inches long enough that the ape could never reach out and touch him. Still, Robbie started to wobble again, and I strained so hard to hold him up still that I farted. And my squeak was all it took to set George off.

The little mutt dog, fierce and loyal, went from his low, threatening growl into a flurry of crazed barking. George, his hind legs kicking up dust, in his fury, barked so hard that it shot him straight back out behind me, away from between my legs. "Creepers," said Robbie, and wobbled a bit more.

"Stand still," I yelled, desperate not to tumble down under Robbie's wobbling.

That set little George off on another flurry, and finally Butto Sam answered us.

His big hand tightened around the iron band, and he let loose a roaring bellow while he shook the whole cart. George's little barking either stopped or disappeared into the big ape's bellow. Robbie threw one of his hands back to get clear, and he twisted sideways on my shoulders. He had only his one palm touching the cart, and the rest of him was flying free.

And then it came. Inside that white metal box, Butto Sam the Highland Gorilla from the Islands beyond the Cape of Lost Hopes reared back and struck the walls of his cage, whether it was with a foot or his free hand we'll never know. But the force of his blow sent a shiver through the whole cart, through Robbie's one palm on the wall, through my hands clutching the cart tire. And that wooden cart covered with fiberglass and corrugated steel thrummed like a tympani being beaten. And for the first time I wondered how something so frail and jimmied together could hold him.

Out of the corner of my eye, as I held onto the cart wheel and gazed up at the ape's tight fist grasping an iron bar in his cage, I saw Robbie come tumbling backwards off of my shoulders, his bifocals flying off somewhere in the grass. The great black ape pounded the walls, bellowing and barking, so I couldn't believe this little enclosure could possibly hold him now. We had done it. We were in honest to God trouble now. The loss of Robbie's weight on my shoulders, along with the trembling of the cart wheel in my hands, and I suppose if I'm honest, the quaking of my own knees, seemed to lift me right off the ground. Maybe it was just that I jumped in the air. I don't remember. But I know I lost my hold on the cart. I wound up on my ass, tangled up in the squirming legs of my little brother, pushing his kicking shoes away from my face, with George standing on my chest now, barking bravely still up at the roaring Butto Sam.

The little white cart rocked from side to side on its wheels, and the long red Buick it was hitched to bounced on its rear shocks. And Butto Sam bellered and brayed like a mule now, and then like a hound, and finally like every beast in the dark woods I'd ever imagined.

"Calma!" sang out a deep voice from somewhere. "Calma, Sammy." It resonated with the pounding of Butto Sam's steel and fiberglass tympani. Deep and full, it took a third singing out, "Calma, mi' Butto! Silenzio!" before the great ape fell silent.

7

And that silence, though it lasted for just a moment, it was just a pause really before little George started to growl again. And yet that silence was stunning. The uproar of Butto Sam was gone, though in the moment before it had obtained the world and pummeled it all into low submission, but now it was gone. Gone at the just call of a voice.

"Geez," said Robbie, in the pause.

Little George growled up at the big hand still resting in the window up above us. And then I heard, from behind me, the crinkle of wheels in the dry grass.

I got hold of George by his red collar and pulled myself up out of Robbie's shoes, "It's okay, George, boy. Shhhh," I said to the growling dog. I wish I could say that George went quiet the way the ape had, at the sound of my command. He just growled on and on, ignoring everything but his brave defense of us, two boys stretched out on the dry grass.

But Butto Sam was completely silent. I flopped around in the dust, still holding George's collar in my one hand. All the horses and that elephant had lifted their heads from their grazing, and they all gazed over at us, munching calmly but staring glassy eyed at my brother and me sprawled out in the grass.

I saw his tall, laced boots first, dark and muddy brown they ran all the way up to his knees, with the laces crisscrossing tight from his toe clear up his shin. They were an impressive pair of boots, boots meant to kick around in the corral, to climb the bald rock face, to stride through jungle thickets or wade the shallow everglade swamps. They were polished and sharp, but not new, for they were old and broken in, and the soles had clearly been replaced, and several times at that. . So it was even more startling as I realized those boots rode on the footrests of a wheelchair.

"Are you lads all right?" the deep voice above those boots said.

George turned away from the silent cage of Butto Sam then, broke free of my grip on his collar, and shot barking toward the man in the chair.

"Calma, Butto," his voice said again, before the ape could even respond to the charging little dog.

I rolled over on my side then and managed to get up onto my hands and knees. Robbie was searching though the grass with his hands for his glasses. I watched as little George charged straight over at the man, though the dog's barking turned into low cautious growls as he grew closer to the wheelchair.

"O piu piccolo," the man said, as his voice softened and he reached an open palm out to the little terrier mutt.

The man in the chair wore some kind of brown pants, almost the color of his tall old boots. On his head he had a little brown pork-pie hat, felt but nearly the color as his boots and pants. And all that brown just set off his shirt.

It was a deep, bright red, blousy and full on him. It was untucked and belted at his waist with a thick brown belt. The blousy sleeves were folded back to leave his thick forearms bare.

"Mi' piccolo," he cooed at the little dog with his baritone, and George went quiet, cocked his head and looked up at the man in the red shirt.

His forearms were truly amazing, I'd never seen any so big before, as thick as a low oak branch, and covered with black hair. And his hand, stretched out to the little dog, was broad and rough. "Mi' piccolo," he said again, and now George stepped forward to sniff his fingertips, and then to lick his palm.

Robbie had retrieved his glasses, and was standing up, turning around, but I was still kneeling in the grass.

"So, little ragazzi, everything okay?" The man said. He wore a red neckerchief, a common red farmers' hanky, around his neck, only a little brighter red than that of his shirt.

"Yup, Mister, " said Robbie, dusting off the seat of his pants. I was still speechless. "We're fine," Robbie chirped.

The man in the chair chuckled a little at that, and sat back. "How 'bout you, boy?" he looked down at me. His eyes were green, and dark under the shadow of his brow. He had a gray stubble of a beard, a couple of day's thick growth on his chin, but it was nearly hidden by the great black mustache he wore. I nodded yes, and stood up, hearing Butto Sam relaxing back farther into his cage behind me.

"Speak up, boy, " the man said. "Non parla inglese? Are you all right?"

"Yeah," I said, and my voice sounded weak and squeaky even to me.

"Don't let the fur grow on your tongue, lad. Speak up!"

Robbie started to laugh at that, and his laughter made the man in the chair grin under that big moustache. "Ah, miei ragazzi! Trying to steal a peek at old Butto Sammy for free, were you?"

I just stood there, afraid to answer. Robbie was the one who chimed out, "But we didn't really see nothing, Mister. I only saw a little bit, like his eyes in the dark, and his fingers. And Willie," he pointed over at me, "he didn't see nothing."

"But you were trying, weren't you?' the man said back, his voice booming and his head cocked forward to glare at us. But I noticed his big hand was scruffing at little George's head now. "Weren't you?" he repeated, when neither Robbie nor me spoke up.

I nodded my head yes.

When Robbie saw me confessing, he piped up again. "It was too dark in there to see anything, Mister. We didn't see nothing worth paying for, not Willie nor me. Nothing."

I was looking over at Robbie, standing there like a little rooster, with grass stuck in the hair at the back of his head, and his striped t-shirt twisted around half sideways on him, and with his bifocal glasses all crooked, and I was thinking we were really in for it now, and he should sure enough shut up.

The man in the wheel chair saw me glaring at my little brother, and he listened to Robbie repeat himself, "Nothing worth paying for, Mister." Then the man broke out in a big bellowing laugh, his eyes moving from Robbie to me and to Robbie again, and then finally they rolled up to the clear summer sky.

"Well, boys, the public has to pay to get a look at Butto Sam, and to see the things that he can do," the man boomed out to the powdery summer clouds above us. "And I'm afraid, O ragazzi, that goes for you Willie, and for you too, my little rooster. What's your name, mi' figlio?"

"Robert," said Robbie, his shoulders pulled back.

"I see," the man said, and he leaned back in his wheelchair. He stopped scruffing at little George's head. With an easy twist of his forearms, he wheeled himself over near Robbie and me. "Willie and Robert," he said, with the air now of a general giving orders softly, because he knew they would be followed.

"Get on home to your mother, you lads, and leave my ape alone. And ask your dear Mama for the coins to come into the Big Top, and then you'll see Butto Sam. But not before, Willie and Robert. Not before, my little ragazzi."

As he spoke, he worked the chair gracefully, herding us away from the cart that held the ape. I skedaddled a good few steps away, past the long red Buick. But not Robbie. He shuffled his shoes in the grass, and moved slowly along, with George beside him, and the man in the chair right behind.

"C'mon, Robbie," I said, "Let's get out of here."

"Robbie, is it?" the man in the wheelchair said. "Bring back some coins tomorrow, little man, and I'll let you shake hands with Butto Sam, Robbie." Then he chuckled that deep laugh in his chest.

Robbie stumbled back a couple of steps, and then said, "So what's your name, Mister. Being that you know mine now." He reached up and pushed his bifocals straight on his nose.

"My friends call me Il Rosso," the man said. "But you can call me Mr. Burton for now, little man. Now go check your mother's purse for some change, Robert the little rooster. And I'll see you tomorrow, Oh piccolo Robbie." And he laughed and laughed at him, and it made me mad.

"C'mon," I said, and got myself a few more steps away. ""Let's get outta here."

"Mr. Burton?" Robbie said, and stood his ground. "You can call me Robert for now."

Burton laughed big at that. "Senza altro, Mr. Robert," he nodded his head. "Signor Robert, it is."

Finally Robbie skipped over toward me, with little George out in front of him. Robbie was grinning wide now, and he pulled his t-shirt around straight as he came.

"Let's get outta here," I repeated.

As we ran down the hill, past the horses and the elephant, we heard Jack Burton's deep voice, carrying over the grass. "Uno momento, mi' Butto! Aspetti! Aspetti!" But we didn't look back to see what the big man in the chair and the big ape in the box were doing. We just ran, to be free and away. We ran, wondering how we'd ask for the money for tomorrow, for the Big Top. And we dreamed as we went of shaking hands with the great black ape, with Butto Sammy, just the way Mr. Burton said that we could.

We ran, hoping against hope and wondering how we could, as we rolled toward home.

The long red Buick was pulled out at the edge of town, in front of the little motel. The joint was just a little strip of five rooms by a gravel parking lot, back from the highway. There was an ancient hotel downtown, but it was filled mostly with several old folks, too frail to take care of themselves. So those five meager rooms of the little motel were it for accommodations in our town. Our house was not far from there. We were neighbors of the Coogans who ran the motel. But Robbie and I were so focused on the ape in his cage, we never noticed the big Buick over there that evening after dinner, as we headed back to the schoolyard and all its foreign magic.

Butto Sam's cart was still up in the schoolyard, but after dark that night, the cage seemed frighteningly quiet. Robbie and I wandered around it, sitting there unhitched now from the big car, but the ape inside was silent. We decided he was asleep in the cooling dusk, but that didn't mean we had stopped wanting to see him. The elephant was great, and we'd seen a lot of nice horses around here before. But the ape, I think it was mostly that he was hidden from our sight that made him so much more important even that that giant elephant in our school grounds. We ran round the cart for a while, singing softly "Zambooti! Zambooti! Who's afraid-a ole Zambooti?" Still the cart returned only silence to our singsong play, so we slowly sang it louder and louder. But there was nothing.

I stopped when I noticed something sprouting out of the side of the cart. It was a long piece of hose like the one from our mother's vacuum cleaner, and it ran all along the steel bars that made the hitch to pull the cart behind that long smooth Buick. "What is it?" Robbie said.

"How do I know?" I pulled it and Robbie took the end and sang through it in his deepest voice, which wasn't all that deep, "Zambooooooooti Sam!" Still not a sound from the sleeping beast.

Finally I took a stick and scratched at the wall of the cart, and the corrugated steel made a rattling sound. Still, there was no response. So I stuck the tip of that stick through the iron bars of the ape's window. Nothing.

"He's not in there," I decided.

"Then where is he?" Robbie said, not really believing me. He walked up to the walls of the cart and drummed on them with his fists, trying to make it sound like the tympani that Butto Sam had played that afternoon. "Hey! Butto! Come out and play!" Robbie bellered, imitating with his little voice the booming baritone of Mr. Burton. But it was just a little rat-a-tat-tat and the squeaking of a kid, and all it got was the blank gazes of the horses and the elephant pegged around the school grounds.

"He's not in there," I said again.

"Then where is he?" Robbie still couldn't believe that this giant ape might be loose and free in our town.

I shrugged.

"Maybe he's escaped." Robbie started to grin with excitement. "He's out wandering in the wood, down by the river." Then he giggled a little.

"Maybe," I said, as I walked around the cart and touched the latch on the rear door. "But if he's escaped, he was clever enough to lock the door behind himself."

Robbie looked at me for a minute, then he looked at where the long red Buick had sat. "He's with Mr. Burton, " Robbie said.

I nodded yes, and that was the beginning of our search for the red Buick. It wasn't hard, in our little town, for two kids to make the rounds in an evening. So we got little George and we started our quest, and we walked from one end of the town to the other. George scurried out ahead of us, sniffing at the ground, peeing on the bushes and curbs and having a great old time.

It seemed like a long while then, but I suppose in a half hour or so we came upon the car. It was parked right where we had started out from home that night. It was tucked straight and neat, directly in front of the last room in the motel, the room that was farthest away from the motel's office. That was good, because it gave us a way to sneak around the back and not be seen.

First, Robbie and I searched around the red car, long and massive with its smooth, rounded curves and big chrome fenders. "He's keeping Butto Sam in the car," Robbie whispered, "I betcha." We crawled around to the rider's side of it, so we couldn't be seen by anyone down at the office. We crept closer and closer like a pair of thieves, while little George just strolled up and peed on the front tire.

"There's nobody in there," I said.

We peered inside, under the white soft top, at the red leather interior with its white trim. There was a leather jacket in the back seat, and an army green blanket, but other than that the car was empty.

"Look at that shifter," Robbie whispered. There were a pair of hand controls where the shift stick should have been. They were steel and parallel and shot up from the floor of car. The "T" handles on their ends were worn a smooth gray, different than the shine and polish of the other chromed controls in that beautiful automobile.

"That's no shift stick," I said. "This is an automatic on the column, see, Robbie?" I pointed to the white stick on the column by the steering wheel, and the ivory PRNDL written on the dash beneath the curved speedometer.

"Then what are those things?"

15

"I don't know. I never saw anything like them," I said.

But at the same moment we both spotted the linkage that led down to the Buick's floor pedals. "That one's the gas," Robbie whispered.

"And the other's the brakes."

"Wow," he said a little too loudly. I shushed him, but I didn't need to, for he whispered, "Pretty neat."

We stared at those hand controls for a while, I guess letting the realities of what life is like in a wheelchair sink into our young heads. But then Robbie was the one who got us back on track. "Where you think that big monkey is, Willie?"

I looked over at the screen door to motel room #5. It was a warm summer night, but behind that screen, the metal inside door was closed tight. And now George was over there, sniffing at the corners of the screen.

"He must have taken it in there," I said.

"Let's go see," Robbie slipped away from the rider's side of the car before I could answer, and crept around to the backside of the motel. I followed behind him, staying low to the ground. Little George looked up from the screen door and then scampered along behind me.

There was a window at the back of the motel room, open but with the shades drawn, so all we could see was the light glowing inside. "You think he's in there?" Robbie said, but he didn't need to ask. We both stuck our noses up against the screen, trying to peer through the curtain, praying for a little summer breeze to lift them and let us see inside. But they were prayers without an answer. The heavy curtains hung as limp as if they were wet.

In one lower corner the screen wire had rusted brown. Robbie looked at me, grinned, and then pushed two of his fingers right through the weakened screen. "What are you doing?" I whispered at him. He just grinned and shrugged his shoulders at me.

George began growling low again. We both glanced back at the little dog, to see what was upsetting him. Down at the bottom of the hill below us, I saw Mrs. Coogan, the owner of the motel, strolling along across her yard enjoying the summer evening. "Shhh," I said to Robbie, and pointed down at her, at what I thought George was growling at. And then, while we weren't watching, out of my peripheral vision, I saw the curtains part.

Slowly, it seemed, and silently, the ape's great black face peered out at us through the screen. We froze for a moment, and even George was quiet behind us. Then, at the same moment, Butto Sam reached a paw up to touch Robbie's fingers in the screen, to the accompaniment of George's low growl. It was just an instant in the still summer night, until it all exploded. But I stood, unable to move, watching it all happen.

At the touch of Butto Sam's paw, Robbie screamed and recoiled away from the window, dragging his two fingers out of the screen, falling backward onto the ground. The aluminum window frame thrummed like an autoharp in the quiet night air. George leapt out of the way of Robbie's fall, and then leapt up onto my brother's stomach, from where he began to bark and bark up at the ape in the window. Butto Sam let out a loud startled grunt, not frightened, but quizzical. Down in the yard below, Mrs. Coogan bellowed out, "Hey, you kids!" and shifted up from the stroll to a waddle, racing her way toward us. "What are you kids doing up there?"

Inside the motel room, back past the ape's face, I saw Mr. Burton in his chair. His brown hat was off, and he had bare white feet sitting on the footrests of the wheelchair. But he still wore that bright red shirt. He had a bottle of some hard yellow liquor in his hand, and he was clearly just finishing a swallow. The hair on his head was the same gray and white stubble as what sprouted on his chin, and the whole of that stubble just made the great fur of his moustache seem larger and thicker and blacker.

"Butto," he yells, and pointed at him with the half empty bottle. "Silenzio" George kept up his yapping bark, as Butto Sam silently moved away from the open window and let the curtain fall back into place.

Robbie was on the ground, crying a little but trying to hold it in. His fingers were bleeding from the screen wire, and he was gazing at them, sniffing. But I think his tears were more about his fears than that little blood on his knuckles.

"Let's get out of here, Robbie," I said, bending down and grabbing his arm to pull him up. It didn't do me any good to leave Robbie behind, because I figured if Mrs. Coogan got to one of us, she got us all. In a little town like ours, everybody knew who you were and who you belonged to. "C'mon," I said, almost lifting Robbie up on his feet by just tugging at his free hand. The other hand he still had stuck in his mouth, to stop the bleeding, or to stop the crying, I'm not sure which.

George turned some of his barking toward Mrs. Coogan then, but he still yapped a few up at the window now and then too, just to make sure the ape knew his place.

Once I had Robbie up and moving, I turned and headed around the backside of the motel. Robbie was only a few steps behind. As we rounded the next corner, leaving Mrs. Coogan far behind us we thought, we sprinted toward the gravel parking lot and the long red Buick. That would be our way out of the neighborhood, I figured. It gave us something to duck under and hide behind, if we needed it, until we could slip away into the dark of falling night.

Little George barked and snarled once more up at the window, before he shot around the corner behind us and then roared past us in a sprint. Up ahead, he disappeared around the corner of the motel where all the doors to the rooms were waiting. We heard him bark once, and then he was quiet. And that was strange enough to slow me down. I could see the tail fins of the Buick out in the lot ahead of us, past the last corner. But I pulled up to a stop at the edge of the corner, and waited, listening to see what was happening, waiting to hear something from noisy little George that would let us know what lay waiting around the corner. But Robbie, a few steps behind me and with those fingers still in his mouth, just ran straight past me and right around the corner, into whatever was there, and I couldn't yell at him to stop, we were to close to whatever was waiting with George on the other side. So I pressed up flat against the white slate siding of the motel, and waited to see what happened next.

"Hi," I heard Robbie say meekly, sounding startled.

And then there was more quiet.

There should have been a bark or something out of George, and surely somebody should have answered Robbie. But there was nothing for the longest moment. I tried to imagine what had happened to the little dog and my baby brother. If they'd fallen in a hole, or into a policeman's grasp, or even into the jaws of an enraged Butto Sammy, there should at least have been a little yelp before they disappeared. But there was nothing. And that was really frightening.

So after a moment of listening and waiting, I cautiously leaned over and tried to peek around the corner to see what had happened. But the sight of just the top of my head was greeted by a deep baritone laugh, and so I pulled back against the corner hideaway, having seen nothing. That laugh though could only belong to the big man in the wheelchair.

19

"Come out, Willie," Robbie yelled far too loudly. "It's okay." Then George gave out a happy little yip. It vanished into the deep rolling laughter.

So I stepped slowly out around the corner to find Mr. Burton sitting in front of the closed door to his room, with George resting happily up in his lap getting scruffed around his collar, and with my little brother standing beside them both, grinning with his two fingers stuck back in his mouth again.

But over Mr. Burton's shoulder, not too far past this happy and contented little scene, I could see the top of the stairs that led up to the motel. Before I could digest what I saw, before I could mutter a weak hello to the laughing man, Mrs. Coogan at full throttle crested the top of the stairs, arms pumping and head bobbing from her exertion.

"William and Robert," she bellowed, and barked out last names out too. "You boys stay right there!" We must have looked to her like were ready to bolt.

Mr. Burton's laughter died away, and with one hand he wheeled himself around so his back was to the closed door of his room.

"Stay right where you are," she yelled in a whisper, remembering now she was running outside the doors to all those guest rooms of her motel. George let out a low growl in her direction, but Burton scratched the dog's chest, and muttered, "Easy, mi' cane, easy," and George was quiet. There was not one sound from behind the door at Mr. Burton's back, where all of us but Mrs. Coogan knew a great African gorilla from the darkest Zambutti lurked waiting. Mrs. Coogan could not know what danger she was in, and I wondered if I should rightly warn her. But that night Butto Sammy was a wonderfully silent great African gorilla.

Mrs. Coogan came to a stop just a few steps away from us. "Good evening, Mr. Burton," she said, sounding obsequious. "I hope these boys haven't disturbed you."

Burton didn't answer right away. He looked over at me, looked deep in my eyes, and then he sent the same calm gaze toward Robbie. Neither of us spoke up. We had him, by the gorilla, so to speak, and everybody there except Mrs. Coogan knew it. But neither Robbie nor I said a word.

"These boys?" Burton said, and turned his mock surprise at the motel keeper. "My two little friends here?" His big hand reached over and rested on Robbie's shoulder.

"I saw them," Mrs. Coogan reared her head back on her shoulders and looked down her plump button nose at all of us. "They were out behind your room, Mr. Burton." And she leaned forward to point at me, ignoring Robbie and our dog beside the man in the wheelchair. "Where they should not have been. And where they're old enough to know better than to be sneaking around." That last part was punctuated with a couple of thrusts of her index finger straight at my heart.

"Oh, these are my friends, Ma'am," Burton smiled up at her from under his great moustache. "Mi' amici piccoli!" he sang in his baritone. "They weren't disturbing me, Ma'am, they were just up for a visit with the circus man. Right? Boys?"

Robbie nodded silently, and I guess I did too.

Mrs. Coogan just made a loud "Harrumph!" through that little nose she was gazing down at us from, and then she looked up at the roof of her motel for a moment, hoping to find some answer there, I guess.

George growled a little again, as it seemed the dog was growling at the motel keeper, but I think he heard something from inside that room, some low movement from the great ape lurking inside, something too soft and animal for our ears to hear. I realized again Mrs. Coogan was in

21

some danger she didn't recognize. Little did she know that the beast of the jungle was waiting as quietly as a predator for her to make the wrong move, to become the hopeless, trapped prey, just the other side of that cheap motel door. Again I felt in some way compelled to warn her, but at the some time I didn't want to give Burton up. I think now that moment held the first great decision of my life: to save the official and obsequious or to protect the unknown and the wild.

I knew of course what I was supposed to do. I knew the right thing to do. I needed to save the small town and the local from the great threat of the outside. It was my duty to get that strange danger and ferocity safely under lock and key, and to control the wild and rescue the order of the everyday.

But at that moment the everyday was squat and wide and wearing a polka dot summer dress, and what's more, it looked down its nose at us.

That very moment, I think, was the real beginning of my life long search for Jack Burton, Il Rosso, the lost and long forgotten Red Shirt. Once I decided to leave Mrs. Coogan hanging there, with her nose in the air, just some unknowing bait before the great beast, the direction of all the rest of my years was sealed and delivered. And my search to find Jack Burton, the real Jack Burton, had begun. But of course, I didn't know any of this then. I was just keeping a secret. Dangerous, yes, but still just a secret.

Burton gently placed that large hand of his on George's head, encircling it with his fingers. "Calma, calma," he whispered as he pulled the dog's ears down softly with just his left hand. George's tongue hung out in a smiling pant and he turned his head and looked up at Mr. Burton lovingly. "Piu piccolo, calma," Burton whispered to him again. I knew somehow he was whispering to the beast behind the door as well.

Mrs. Coogan drew in a great, exasperated breath, and then she began with her orders. "William. Robert. You boys head on home now." Her glare moved from me to Robbie and then back again. The weight of her sentence landed on that final word, "Now." Robbie nodded yes at her, but he didn't move away from Mr. Burton's arm still resting on his shoulders. "I'll be calling to talk with your mother about this. You know you are supposed to say away from . . . " Mrs. Coogan paused, not out of some second thought, but in order to make her point to Burton, sitting there with his arm still around the child. " . . . these circus people," she finished, now glaring at the man in the wheel chair.

She pulled Robbie from Burton's grasp them, and herded us away from him. We scuffled a few steps into the gravel parking lot, never looking away from the man in the red shirt sitting in the wheelchair.

"Come to the circus tomorrow, O ragazzi," Burton called out to us, smiling. "I think we can get you inside." Then he winked at both of us.

That wink made us partners of his. Robbie looked over at me and grinned, because he understood that too, and then he looked back at the man in the wheelchair. We were all together, Burton and Robbie and I, accomplices now together, concealing that great ape hidden just behind the door, we knew, just out of reach of the everyday, lurking just out of the quotidian sight.

Mrs. Coogan reached over and pulled little George out of Burton's lap and set the dog on the ground. His tail twitched and the little black dog looked back up at the man in the chair. "Go on," Mrs. Coogan shooed at George with the back of her hand. "Scoot," she said. George skittered back a step or two in the rocks and weeds toward where Robbie and I were standing in the gravel, but he was still facing Burton, and his tail still twitched in anticipation of something.

But Mrs. Coogan was done with us. As far as she was concerned, we knew what we were supposed to be doing, we'd been given our orders and put back on the safe and narrow path, the direction home. There was nothing more to deal with us. Even though we all three still stood in the gravel next to the red Buick watching, we were already gone home in her eyes. If she'd turned around and looked at the three of us, I think she'd been surprised to see us still there.

Instead, she put her fists on her polka dot hips and turned toward the wheelchair. "Now, Mr. Burton, sir, we've got some things to talk about," she said.

"See you tomorrow, mi' boys," Burton said with a wave of his hand that freed us to leave somehow, forced us to go really. "A domani," he yelled, "ragazzi!" And so we scurried away and left him in the clutches of that polka dot dress.

That night, in our twin beds in the dark, Robbie said to me, "Are you sleeping, Willie?" I was wide awake, my eyes wired open with excitement, my heart still beating fast at the prospect of going to the circus tomorrow. Of really seeing Butto Sam, not through some window or curtain or brace of bars. But just there, the whole of him, in all his wildness and power. But I knew if I answered, we would both be up all night, squirming and whispering at one another. And it would become a long, long night. It would take until forever for the sun to rise and the day of the circus to dawn. So I didn't answer my brother. It was the only way to make tomorrow come sooner. And though it took a long while, I heard Robbie sleeping eventually, and I never let on I was awake. Somehow, in a dark that I can't remember, I slept too.

*   *   *

The next day, the circus day, was hard with disappointment. There had been a phone call from Mrs. Coogan, of course, and then there was a lot of explaining that needed to be done, and that we couldn't do. And that, shortly, was the end of all hope. The world of Zambutti and the African Islands and their darkest reaches, of elephants and plumed white horses, was suddenly only a distant dream.

Little George never came around and the edges of our lawn were trimmed and squared, and every little dandelion was dug out, root and all. And not just the flowering ones, but every one, every leaf we could find, and some besides that were pointed out to us. And then there was a garage to sweep and hedges to trim, and then a set of twin beds changed and turned and dusted and vacuumed.

And so it grew dark, and all the circuses were miles away, forever and unjustly traveling away from us. And Butto Sam was just a name written in red on some remembered wall, nothing better than an illusion, a word in a dusty library book no one reads anymore.

At the end of it all, of that horrid, long day, we were confined to our room. Sent to the prison with twin beds we'd been forced to dust and clean all day while our friends and mates went to the magic world of the Circus of Butto Sammy, seeing all the marvels we would hear about again and again in the days to come, but never see. But never know.

The world was a cruel place on that day of the traveling circus.

Still, while our dreams may have been imprisoned, our spirits indeed ran free.

In the darkest of dark of night, I slipped out of my bed. I saw Robbie buried in the tumble of covers and pillows in the bed across from mine. Silently, I pulled on my heavy corduroy trousers and with my shoes and with a cap on my head, I slipped over to the window. Even I was amazed at my own silent stealth, because Robbie never once even rustled around.

The screen was so easy to shift out of place that it popped loose and clattered down into the soft grass outside the window. At the noise of the screen I froze, and only slowly turned back to look at Robbie's still form lying in the bed. I expected to see him sitting up, rubbing his eyes and looking at me vaguely in the dark, trying to see without his glasses. And then I would have to take him along, we'd have to run away together and all of my escape would be slower, and with bifocals, and probably impossible. And all because of a window screen flopping down into the summer grass.

I heard a soft, "Shhhh!" behind me.

Remember, I was turned back, looking over at Robbie's little form stretched out on his bed, waiting for him to sit up. The window to freedom was at my back. And that "shhh!" behind me came from outside.

It made me jump, and I twisted back away from the open window, and fell on my bum on the hardwood floor with a thump. Out the window I saw nothing but the stars and the swash of the Milky Way in the sky.

Then Robbie's head popped up inside the window. "Will," he whispered so quietly I barely understood him, "you're going to get us caught." Then his head disappeared into the dark outside again.

I sat there for a moment, my butt on the floor, resting back on the palms of my hands behind me, staring at my black Converse tennis shoes out in front of me, and listening to my heart beat in my ears.

Then Robbie's head, in his Cub's cap, floated up into the window from the dark outside again. "Will! Are you coming?" Robbie said. "Or are you staying home?"

I glanced back over my shoulder at the lifeless clump of bedding in Robbie's bed, still half expecting it to sit up and speak some sense to me.

"But you're not getting us caught," Robbie's disembodied head outside in the dark said at me. It paused a moment, then a little disembodied hand rose up and pushed the bifocals up on his nose.

"C'mon," Robbie whispered. And then disappeared.

I clambered back up onto my feet, and then realized if I wasn't silent I would wake up the whole house, and the great escape would be over. So with a new resolve to be quiet, I crawled out the open window and hopped down into the grass next to the screen.

Robbie emerged out of the shadows of an elm tree, out near the highway. He lifted up an arm and waved me onward and over to him, and then like some resistance fighter in the night, he disappeared back into the dark of the elm.

I scurried over to the tree, and found him there waiting. "Let's go," he whispered. He reached down and hefted up a little olive green rucksack, tossed it over one shoulder and straightened his cap.

His clothing was all dark and he wore the dirt brown jacket to his snowsuit, even in the warmth of the summer night. He slipped away across the highway and headed toward the other end of town, moving from tree to tree quickly.

It took only a moment to catch up with him, because I was wearing my most heavy cords and a sweatshirt, with my fastest Connie's on my feet. And I wasn't lurking at every tree, looking both ways, and then darting to the next tree. I just upped my heels and licked it, running full bore across the highway and then down the sidewalk. Speed was my key, not deceit.

I caught up with him by an old elm, three houses down the street. "Hey," I said, "where are we going?" I looked down at his feet and noticed he was wearing his Sunday church shoes, the brown ones with wingtipped toes. But you couldn't see the wingtips, because they were covered with his hand-me-down rubbers, the brown ones I used to "forget" at the schoolhouse so I didn't have to wear them, even though they had Hop-a-long Cassidy buttons on the side. Since I wouldn't wear them, and he grew into them, so Robbie inherited those rubbers from me.

"I'm going to join up with Mr. Burton," Robbie said. "Ill-a-Rose-o!" he whispered, imitating the deep sound of Burton's voice, as he followed my eyes down to the rubbers on his feet. "How about you?" Robbie asked, as he scuffed his heel in the grass to show off how well he was prepared. "Are you coming too?" He hefted one of the straps on his backpack up higher on his shoulder. "You didn't bring your stuff, Will."

I looked down at his face and saw that the edges of his hair were damp with sweat. "I don't know about that," I said.

Robbie nodded his head at me, as if he knew that I wouldn't have the guts to go through with it. I just wanted to see the circus, that was all I was good for. This is what his eyes said to me.

"Why don't you let me carry that," I said, putting my hand on that little khaki sack.

He stared at me, getting ready to object.

"Ill-a-Rose-o!" I whispered, making my voice into the deepest baritone I could.

Robbie gazed at me for a long moment, then with a nod of his head, he slipped the rucksack off his shoulders and handed it to me. Maybe he was hoping I would join in the adventure, maybe he didn't want to risk it all alone. Maybe he just trusted me to join in, or maybe it was just that he was tired and hot from running in a winter coat through the summer night. But he handed me his bag and then he wiped his damp brow on the sleeve of his coat.

"I think I'll just carry this," he said, and slipped the heavy coat off.

His rucksack was heavy and hard as metal, and when I slipped it onto my shoulder it dug into my lower back with some sharp edges inside. But I didn't say anything about it, or I knew he'd take it back. "Ill-a-rose-o!" I said louder, and Robbie grinned at me, holding his coat in his arms. He had a wool sweater on under the coat, and beneath that I saw my old boy scout shirt, the one I always used for camping out.

"Ill-a-rose-o!" Robbie said.

And then we were off at a sprint to the edge of town. We came around the back way, by the alleys, to the rear of the motel, and there we found a light on in Mr. Burton's window. We'd made it this far by staying away from the main drag all through town, so we never even thought of going around to the front of the motel, under the lights of the gravel lot, and knocking on the man's door. That was no way for two young adventurers to approach the doorway to our destiny.

No, we crept quietly up to that lit rear window, watching always and everywhere for Mrs. Coogan to be lurking about. But the night was dark and moonless, with great broken clouds now moving over the stars and across the Milky Way. Mr. Burton's window was open and the night breezes had parted the curtains. This was the way to begin the story of our adventures.

I put my finger up to my lips, and Robbie nodded. Then I pulled his heavy rucksack off my back, and carried the lunk of it under my arms. Together we slunk up to the window, staying low and out of sight.

We both remembered Butto Sammy greeting us in that window, startling us onto our backsides, so we were careful and quiet this time. Robbie stayed crouched on the ground beneath the window. While I slowly stuck my head up to look inside, Robbie kept the cautious watch for Mother Coogan, who might still be roaming around.

Slowly I peeked up through the screen, and I couldn't believe what I saw inside. At first I just sensed someone moving around in the room, under the yellow lights of the ceiling bulb. Then a little brush of wind slipped past my ear and lifted the curtains up away from the window. They fluttered just a touch, before they drooped back down, but in that instant I saw them.

And I'd never seen anything like them before. What I expected, of course, was the man in his chair and that great ape of his, the one I'd still not gotten a straight look at for all my trying, lumbering around the room somewhere. Instead, I saw them.

The taller one was wearing only her panties, and her back was toward me, as she ran both her hands up through her long tussle of bright red hair. Her friend was sitting on the edge of the bed, wearing a little baby blue robe that hung open and draped down around her onto the bed. She had a

30

cigarette in one hand and she turned her head, drew in a long draught of tobacco. Then slowly she tilted her head back and blew the smoke out through her ruby painted lips. The tilt of her head and the movement of her arm away with the cigarette opened up that thin robe and showed me the nothing beneath it, and especially it showed me the triangle of black hair in her lap.

It might be the air I sucked in, but whatever it was, the breeze died and the curtains fell back down in place. I dropped down on the ground, with my back against the motel wall and sat by my brother.

"What is it?" he whispered.

But I couldn't speak. I just sat still and tried to keep my eyes from bugging out, because they felt at that moment like I might never shut them again.

"Ill-a-rose-o?" Robbie whispered.

I swallowed. I shook my head no. Then I turned around again and stuck my head up there for another look.

They were talking softly to one another, and I could see only that the red-haired one was walking around while the one in the amazing blue robe sat and smoked. But I couldn't see in, because those curtains hung thick and dense and still, heavy as stones in a doorway. And in the summer air there was not now even a hint of a breeze.

But it was summer, and I knew the breeze would come suddenly, and at some time, at some moment, the one with the red hair would turn around. I shifted side to side a little, trying to peek through any curve in the curtains, all to no avail.

They spoke back and forth to one another something I couldn't hear, and then the redhead sang a little bit of some song. Robbie, on the ground beside me, whispered, "Will, who is it?"

I just shushed him and gestured with my hand for him to stay down and keep a look out. But I didn't move from my place, waiting for that sweet summer breeze to shake open my world again.

I wasn't paying much attention to Robbie. I was focused on my next glimpse through the screen. So I didn't notice him slowly standing up, like a commando, with his back to the window, still the good lookout. When he was up straight, and standing on the opposite side of the window, he threw a quick glance over his shoulder at the window.

Inside the two women were laughing now, and Robbie looked over at me with big eyes of his own. With two short waves of my hand, I gestured him to get down but he wasn't paying any attention. I realized then that, unlike me, there was deep disappointment in his face. He'd come here planning to run away on an adventure with the deep voiced man in the chair and his great ape companion. It was the beginning for Robbie of his great escape. Instead he found his hero tangled up with a couple of "girls."

But me, one peep through those curtains at the black dream down in her lap, and I'd completely forgotten about Burton and his monkey. I was having trouble breathing and holding my breath in anticipation at the same time.

But not Robbie. With his back against the motel wall, he pushed up his bifocals on his nose and then scanned the horizon like a trooper preparing to move. Then he cast his head to the side and called out over his shoulder, into the screen and the open window and through the dead, drooping curtains.

"Mr. Burton, are you in there?"

I guess he was going to save the hero from damnation, and get us all rolling on our real journey. There was no time for this dallying around with women.

I know I winced, and sunk down into the ground, and there was a soft scream from one of the women inside. Robbie just stood with his back flat against the wall, hidden from view by anyone who might look out through the window.

"Mr. Burton, sir?" he called out again.

I heard scurrying footsteps inside the room and then saw a stream of smoke shoot through the screen above me. It had to be the one in little blue robe at the window. "Who's out there?" she said, and the light behind her in the room switched off so there was only a strong but indirect light coming from the bathroom inside.

I didn't say anything; I was just frozen in place beneath the window. I heard her suck in another toke on the cigarette, and then behind her the other woman, the red head, whispered, "Who is it, Shirley?"

Another stream of smoke flowed out through the screen, as Shirley said, "Billy, is that you? If that's you I'm gonna kill you."

Right then all the stories I'd been told about the wild wandering lives of circus people welled up in me, like a flooded basement of fears under my feet. The thievery, the pick pocketing, the conning you out of your hard earned money, the money you worked for at honest jobs, not flim-flam work like theirs. The knife fights and the gambling, and the dancing dangerous music under dark lights in unspeakable clothes. And yes, the stealing of children.

All those stories, gathered up in just a few years of living from generations and generations of hate and distrust, they were there beneath me, like rising water in a cloud burst. So I hung low to the ground, out of the sight of that window, just as I thought Robbie would. And I began to think quickly of where and how to bolt off into the dark, searching for ways of escape.

But right then Robbie, with a determined look in his eyes, stepped out from the wall and faced the window, stepped into the pale, indirect light it cast out onto him.

Shirley in the blue robe gasped at his deliberate move in the dark. She was startled, but she didn't drop the curtain.

"We're looking for Mr. Burton, ma'am," Robbie said.

"Jack?" Shirley said, incredulous.

"Who is it, Shirley?" the red head's voice came from deeper inside the room. "Is it that boyfriend of yours?"

"You're looking for Jack?" Shirley of the robe said.

"Could you get Mr. Burton for us, please?" Robbie said.

"Is it Billy?" I heard the pad of the red head's bare feet coming toward the window across the linoleum floor.

"It's just some little kid," Shirley said. "What's your name, kid?"

"Never mind that, ma'am," said Robbie. "We need to talk to Mr. Burton."

"We?" said the redhead from behind Shirley.

"Who's we?" said Shirley.

I saw the redhead's face poke out into the light from the screen, so I plastered myself up against the wall even closer, if that was possible.

"Billy, are you out there?" said Shirley of the robe. "If you put some pint assed kid up to this, I'll hang your hide on these walls in here." She drew in a long, hot tug on her cigarette, so I hard a toke I could hear the little cigarette pop in her hand as she drew in.

"There's no Billy here," said Robbie, defiant. "It's just me and my brother Will, and we're here to talk to Mr. Burton." He added, "Ma'am," a bit too late.

There was a long silent pause then, followed by the cackling laughter of both women. They both said "Jack" once or twice in the midst of their chuckles.

"Come around to the front door, little man," Shirley of the robe said. "And bring your brother, so we can see you two big boys in the light." Then they cackled a little more, muttering "Jack" back and forth between them.

Robbie looked down at me, the determination solid in the set of his jaw. He didn't nod his head, he didn't say a word, he just shoved the glasses up on his nose one more time and then turned and strutted off around the motel, like a proud warrior headed toward battle formation.

I sat for a moment, feeling my plans and hopes of escape drifting away. The curtain had fallen back down over the window and the lights had come back on inside the room and while I thought about bolting away, I knew I couldn't leave Robbie alone in the clutches of those women, kidnapped by the gypsy caravan. So I stood up and looked inside one more time, because I couldn't resist one last peek. But there was nothing to see. The door across the room was open onto the parking lot, but I knew this only because the curtains were pinned hard against the screen from the breeze flowing across the room now. I couldn't even see their shadows inside, much less any of my dreams.

So I followed Robbie around the motel one more time. He was fearlessly out in front of me again, all his caution thrown by the way. First I noticed what wasn't there. Out in the gravel lot there was no Buick, not a red one or any other kind. Where Burton's great car had sat there was only a Kaiser, pea green where it wasn't rusted out. But there was not even a tire track left behind by the long red Buick convertible, with its silver trimmed wings and its pearl white soft top.

I began to understand, then, that we had not stumbled on some kind of tryst. This was not Mr. Burton entertaining. These two women were certainly the "exotic" dancers from the carnival show, but they had taken Burton's room somehow. They were not guests in the fun I could only then begin to imagine, the magnetic but still mysterious body of joy I could only guess at. There was no scent of anything male in the vicinity, other than my kid brother and me.

The redhead was waiting in the open door to the motel room, wearing now a long flannel shirt, red and brown like her hair. She had her hand on her hip and as Robbie walked boldly over to her, I hung back a ways. It was a mixture of fear and fascination, for that redhead had the fullest lips I'd ever seen, and even under that flannel, shirt I could see the loose shape of her large breasts hanging free.

"Where's Mr. Burton?" demanded Robbie.

"Come on in here, little man," said Shirley's voice from inside the room. "And where's that big brother of yours?"

"He's out here," said the redhead. Then she waved me toward her, "Come on," she said and smiled with those full lips of hers, redder than even Jack Burton's Buick. "We won't bite," she chuckled again.

My feet led me over to the door, while the rest of me was in complete turmoil. As I approached the light in the doorway, with my head down, she put an arm around my shoulder and I saw that her toenails were painted the color of her lips, the color of her shirt, the color of the missing Buick car.

"He's a cutie too," Red said, as we stepped into the room together. I looked up and my eyes were met with two shocks at once. First, Robbie was sitting happily on Shirley's miraculous lap, and she had both her arms wrapped around him. And second Shirley, despite that dark black vision I'd seen down inside her little blue robe, was a bright yellow blonde.

I knew then that we were lost. Both Robbie and I, we were about to disappear into the carnival world, never to return. The dancing girls would whirl us away into some wandering life of elephants and show horses and little skimpy clothes covered with plastic sequins and painted lips. We would live now lost in a world of deep dyed hair and painted moustaches, showing fine under the hard hot lights inside the dark tents. We were lost.

"What do you boys want?" Red said, and her arm dropped from my shoulders. I felt the warmth of her around me fade away, and the room suddenly seemed a cool refrigerator, and me with a fever. She left the motel room door open behind us, the light from the floor lamps cast out onto the rusty Kaiser and the loose gravel.

"We're looking for Mr. Burton," Robbie said from Shirley's lap. "Ill-rose-O!" he said, as if that explained it all.

"This was his room," I muttered, and I saw both Shirley and Red lean forward toward me, trying to hear my shy explanation. "Last night," I added, trying to speak louder.

"Jack?" said Red incredulously.

Shirley sat back and hugged Robbie to her, and then she fluffed at his light brown hair around his ear, and straightened the ball cap on his head. "What do you two little lads want with Jack Burton?" she said.

Robbie struggled a bit against her hug with his shoulders, and I looked down from her long exposed thigh to her knee and then along the line of her calf to see that her toenails were painted flamingo pink.

"We're going to be part of his troupe and train all the gorillas in Zambutti," Robbie explained as if it were soon to be a news flash, just a back page story it was so obvious. But where he'd come up with this whole plan of his was news to me. "He lives with a gorilla, you know, " he said.

That made the two women laugh again, and I saw when Red opened her mouth how crooked and yellowed her teeth were behind those rich, painted lips.

"He invited us to come to the circus today," I said, trying to make some sense for them of this garbled dream of my brother's, though I'm not entirely sure why. I guess the part of me still fascinated by their polished and waxed veneer did not want to seem silly and little like a kid. " But we couldn't get there," I said, leaving out the way we'd been grounded by Mrs. Coogan's report. "So we thought we'd come over here tonight," I said. "He was here, last night."

"He invited you to come to the show?" said Shirley, still not believing us, still toying with the hair under my brother's cap. There was a little line of sweat now cutting down from the dark roots of her blonde hair, and etching a route through the smooth powdery make up on her temple and cheek. I saw the hard wrinkles around her eyes, covered by the powder and with the black lines of her eye makeup. "Why would Jack do that?" Shirley said to Red.

"Because we didn't tell on him," Robbie announced, and then he wriggled out of Shirley's grasp. He stood square in front of her and he straightened his scout shirt and pushed his glasses up as he said, "Mrs. Coogan caught us up here, but we didn't tell on him, that he had a gorilla in his room."

This led to another good laugh from the painted dancing girls, and Shirley uncrossed her long legs enough for me to glimpse down in the secret places again. My eyes had not deceived me through the screen; her blonde hair was as phony as the smooth pink blush on her cheeks and the fat red curl of her lips. But still, the long lines of her legs, like angles of terrifying light under that thin robe, were enchantment itself.

"So you boys are the reason he got tossed out of here," said Shirley as she laughed, and wrapped that blue robe around her lap cavalierly, showing off more than she hid. I know now how practiced that flurry of the robes was, but I couldn't recognize it then. I was too young, and I was soon to be lost.

Both Robbie and I were quiet, because even Robbie didn't know what to say.

"He pulled that cripple thing with the motel lady two days ago, you know," Red said, "and he beat us out of the last room left in this little backwater. She sent us all the way to the city to get a room, because she thought we weren't up to 'her standards.'" That's when Red strolled a step or two over, and closed the motel room door. "You could see it in the old lady's eyes, couldn't you, Shirley?" Red said. "We weren't up to 'her standards,' you know." She slipped over next to me then, and her arm wrapped around me, warm and filled with some strange incredible promise.

"But then here she called us up this morning, at the hotel she sent us to," Shirley leaned over and took Robbie's hands in hers, showing off a lot more of her chest under that little robe. I'm sure I was bug eyed, I know my mouth was dry. "Long distance and everything," Shirley drew Robbie to her lap again, as if they were in a dance.

"'I've got a room for you girls now,' the old lady said on the phone," Red took up the story, imitating Mrs. Coogan's pius, sing-song voice pretty well, and now I felt fingertips at the base of my neck, touching me like little live wires. Shirley gave Robbie a hug, and the tie of that robe fell loose showing us a whole lot more of herself.

"We didn't know 'till later it was Jack's room she had for us. The old lady tossed him out because he was going to be a 'bad influence on these boys.'" Shirley had her arms all wrapped around my little brother again.

"On these boys," Red said and her face came close to my cheek and her thick red lips brushed against my face. "These sweet little boys," she whispered and her breath tickled my ear. Still even through all the fascination her touch held over me, I could smell the acrid scent of her last cigarette, and probably all the cigarettes in her life, in that tickle of breath. It didn't really free me from the electric warmth of her touch, but it kept some small part of me aware of the closed motel door and of the big, loose world outside it.

"Mine's cuter than yours," Shirley said, and she let the corner of her robe fall off her shoulder as she held Robbie tightly. One of her breasts was fully exposed, the round brown nipple pointing up at my brother, and he was squirming now to get loose. That was when Red leaned over to me, showing me the freckled cleavage inside her flannel shirt and kissed me on the cheek.

"Oh, I don't think so," Red said, and she took my right hand and guided it up under her shirt.

"Maybe we aren't up to the old lady's standards," Shirley said with a little laugh. But I couldn't see her anymore, and I barely understood her words. I was gone, and a cutely there at the same time.

"You boys wouldn't tell on us, would you?" Red whispered to me, and my hand was on her breast, drawn like a magnet. The nipple was like a hard bead in my palm, and her red hair was brushing all over my face. All I knew was the deep red hair on my cheeks, and the freckled breast in my hand, until suddenly I heard Shirley groan, "Hey," and Robbie came at me like he was stealing home and I was the catcher with the ball in my hand standing between him and the plate. He just rolled straight into me and shoved me out of Red's embrace. The next thing I knew he had pinned me against the motel door with a narrow shoulder, and with both hands he was fumbling at the doorknob. In a moment the metal door sprang open from my weight against it and Robbie and I tumbled out onto the gravel drive.

Robbie was up on his feet immediately, staring down at me. The night was filled with the laughing of Red and Shirley, as they sat back in the yellowed light of the room. Shirley's robe was down now completely around her waist, tangled with the bedclothes, and Red stood a step or two back from the door, with her one freckled breast gazing out at me. She was slowly wiggling one finger at me, gesturing to me to come back inside. Their laughter seemed to come from everywhere but their red, red lips. "Run, Will," Robbie yelled down at me. He grabbed my arm around the elbow and pulled me onto my feet. I couldn't keep from staring back inside at those dancers smiling out at me, their breasts waiting for me, urging me to come back inside the room, while their soft laughter filled the wide night air. "Will," Robbie started to drag me away, "let's get out of here. C'mon."

I turned to run along with Robbie, but the bent lump in my pants wouldn't let me move anyway except sidewise and crooked, staring back toward that room. So with my little brother out ahead of me, and Red laughing and waving at me in farewell, I limped away past the pea green Kaiser and back into the quiet, small town night.

His tent was pitched at the edge of the school grounds, with the elephant and the white horses staked all around it. The night was quiet except for singing crickets and the occasional snort of a horse, or the elephant flapping its ears. But now and again his deep voice boomed out softly as he sang in some language we didn't understand.

His tall tent glowed a pale yellow in the dark, and we crept closer to it. Someone inside it was walking, and Burton sang a little louder and then stopped. "Ill-a-rose-O!" Robbie mouthed at me so I understood, though he didn't even make a sound. I nodded yes. Then we heard Burton's big laugh.

Bright light leaked out of the seams of the tent, and shadows moved around inside, passing through the light, so large they stretched out to the tent ceilings around the tall posts.

The long red Buick had the top up and closed and it was parked next to the tent. The white trailer of Zambutti Sam was hitched to it now, ready to roll away at any moment it seemed. But for now it sat in the light dimmed by the canvas walls of Jack Burton's tent. And a line ran from one of the tent posts to the antenna of the car. From it hung a few pieces of white clothing, a pair of brown pants, and a cardinal red shirt.

"Ill-a-rose-O!" I whispered this time, letting a tiny sound whisper past my lips. Then with a tilt of my head I gestured a 'Let's go' to Robbie. We walked up to the flap door of the brown canvas tent and, before I could call out, there was a little flurry of movements inside as the shadow's shifted broadly against the door.

"Who's out there?" boomed Mr. Burton. "Announce yourself, stranger."

"Mister Burton?" I said, surprising even myself at how clear and loud my voice was in the night.

"Ill-a-rose-O!" Robbie sang out.

There was silence then for a moment inside the tent. Then we heard Mr. Burton say softly, "Sammy, there."

Suddenly the flap of the tent was pulled back and the warm light from inside flooded out onto Robbie and me, standing in front of the opening. At first all we could see was the dark shape of Mr. Burton in his chair in front of us, dark and featureless as a shadow, with the lantern light behind him.

"Miei ragazzi!!" he boomed, and then he gave forth a great, rumbling laugh.

While he was laughing at us, Burton wheeled himself out of the tent a bit and he gazed this way and that around into the dark schoolyard. One of the horses snorted somewhere. Then, once Jack Burton was satisfied that we were alone, he wheeled himself backwards and off to the side. "Come in, ragazzi," he said, "Come in."

Robbie walked in first, eagerly, that lunk of a backpack over his shoulder, but I followed right behind him. A couple of electric lanterns hung from the peaks at the top of the tent poles and in the center of the room sat a round propane heater, glowing red and warm, even in the summer night. On the other side of it the mountain gorilla rested, unchained, one front paw on his lap and the other on the ground, holding him up as he leaned his bulk on the curled knuckles of other paw. He sat on a low wooden stool, with a piece of Indian carpet draped over part of it. The wooden stool was only about eight inches high, and it's seat was a curved wooden board of dark black wood, so dark it seemed painted though if you looked close you could see the lines of the dark grain in it. Zambutti Sam's stool was worn and old, and the wood was thick and sturdy, so it looked like it would be heavy for a man to lift. Impossible for Robbie or me to do much more than shove it around, and hard to imagine a man in a wheelchair, even one as agile as Burton, would be able to lift it.

As we came inside, Burton spoke to the ape, "Zambutti, indietro." The great ape rose on its haunches, lifted that stool with one hand and moved back further into the tent, making room for the rest of us to sit around that warm heater. He set the stool down softly, with hardly a sound, adjusted the chunk of Indian rug, and then sat again with one paw in his lap, the other on the grassy floor of the tent.

"Sit down, little ragazzi," and Burton gestured to a stretch of rug on the dirt and grass that the gorilla had just left empty.

Robbie and I stood there for a moment, wondering about how close we should get to a loose and free mountain gorilla, bigger than both of us rolled together twice. An ape who could lift that stool with just one hand.

"Sit down, sit down," Burton gestured his hand at that rug. "Come in! Sit down! It's okay!"

Then he looked at us just standing there, and he laughed at us.

"If you boys had come this afternoon, you wouldn't be afraid of old Sammy," he said. Then he rolled his chair over so that he sat next to the great ape, and where he would be between us and Zambutti Sam. "Where were you today? You couldn't come to the circus, my little friends? Even for free?"

The gorilla had a black, flat face and a huge rounded point that rose up from his wrinkled brow, and his small, black eyes kept moving around, looking us up and down. His feet had fingers like his hands, even though they were curled up and tucked lightly under his heavy stool.

"Come in, sit down, ragazzi," Burton said, and waved an open hand at the stretch of rug in front of us. As we came, silently around to that rug, he reached behind himself and pulled out a couple of flat, hard pillows, with tassels at the corners, and tossed them over to us. "Please, my little friends, have a seat. We're sorry, Sammy and I, that you couldn't make it to the big top today. We did look for you, you know."

"Mama wouldn't let us come," Robbie said, as he put his pillow down on the rug and gently set that knapsack of his beside it.

"No circus for her good boys?" said Burton.

I wouldn't have said anything, just let the man in the chair think we had better things to do, important things that kept us away. But Robbie was nearly bursting with outrage and the need to tell it all.

"We got grounded," Robbie said, once he was plopped down on his pillow seat. "'Cause Mrs. Coogan called Mama. She told her we were sneaking around at the motel last night. So we couldn't go. We had to stay in our room and we even had to eat our peas tonight."

"Ah, even your peas, il piccolo?" Burton said, shaking his head back and forth sadly, at the great tragedy of the green peas.

Robbie nodded his head yes, pleased at the shared indignation. Then he explained, "That's why we decided to come with you."

Zambutti Sam made a little snort at that, as if he understood my brother's dream.

"Will and me, Mr. Burton, we've just had it with all that. So we're going with you," Robbie said, and patted his life's belongings in the knapsack beside him. But then he paused and the training of our mother's politeness showed through his earnest eyes. "That is, if you'll take us, sir." He paused impatiently. "You will, won't you, Mr. Burton?"

Jack Burton stroked the white stubble of beard on his chin, and he looked over at Zambutti Sam. The ape shifted a little on his stool, and then shook his head back fiercely, looked up at the center pole of the tent, and snorted one loud, swallowed growl. It seemed like a great affirmation, the beginning of a grand adventure for us all, even to me.

"Ill-a-Rose-O!" Robbie sang out proudly, answering the ape's growl.

This brought a little smile to Burton's lips, but he didn't laugh, and he didn't really answer.

"I've had about enough of that Mrs. Coogan myself," he said, leaning forward in his chair and nodding at Robbie. "With all of her nosing around and complaining at me. That's why you find me here, tonight, ragazzi. I moved out of there, I did, and back into this old tent, me and ol' Butto Sammy. We like it better here anyway, it's more like home,

45

though we do miss the plumbing. So we left her little softheaded inn. Ah, the tent and the road, the only things you can trust in this world. That's where we belong, my boys. We don't need any more 'Missus Coogans' hanging around, do we, my little ragazzi cari?"

I found myself nodding yes, along with Robbie. But the pillow underneath me was hard and the schoolyard dirt was scattered all across the Indian rug at me feet, deadening the warm colors in the lamplight.

Then Robbie piped up, "But them girls told us Mrs. Coogan kicked you out." He looked up from his seat into Burton's face, and then over at the great ape. "And not 'cause of Butto Sammy, they didn't know nothing about him 'cause we never told. Did we, Will? We never told nothing." Robbie sat up straight, and looked back at me for verification. "And them girls, they didn't know nothing about Butto Sammy, no sir, Mr. Burton. They said you got thrown out 'cause of Will and me."

Robbie sank back down on the pillow, like the wind had dropped from his full sail ahead dreams. "You got grounded too, Mr. Burton. Just like Will and me." He stared down at Burton's still feet on the rests of the wheelchair, and it was enough to break anyone's heart to see him, all flat and dejected.

So I spoke up, for the first time really, about our running away. And I did it by saying only that one mysterious word, just a nonsense word to us, a magic incantation. "Ill-a-Rose-O!" I said.

Robbie looked up from the dirt floor at me, and then over at Burton in his chair, with the mountain gorilla beside him.

"Well, mi' piccolo povero," Burton said, "I'd say we've had about as much as we can take of all of that. Am I right? For this day, anyway?"

"Ill-a-rose-O!" Robbie whispered.

Burton grinned at that, maybe because we mispronounced it, maybe because we didn't know what we were saying. "Besides, O ragazzi," he said. "I tell you I'd had enough of the old lady Coogan and her nosing around. I left that half-bit hotel of hers on my own, boys. So now, who are you going to believe, a couple of dancing sirens wearing nothing but dusty sequins they can hardly shake anymore, or your old pal, Il Rosso?"

"Ill-a-Rose-O," we muttered in answer together, still trying to imitate the music of his words. But then, furtively, Robbie glanced over at me and it told me all I needed to know. Like me, the story that Shirley and Red told us, it fit a whole lot closer to what we knew of Mrs. Coogan, than what Mr. Burton was trying to say.

But our doubts didn't really matter, because we wanted to believe in Jack Burton. And somehow, because we knew that whether Mrs. Coogan had thrown him out, without ever knowing about Butto Sam, or whether Jack Burton had packed up and left of his own accord, it amounted to the same thing. And that same thing felt a whole lot more like what had happened to us, two boys who couldn't go to the circus, grounded in their room with nothing but chores and cleaning up to look forward to for all of time ahead, as far to the fore as we could see. And that tent, with its lantern light and its free ranging gorilla, whether Mr. Burton was lying or not, was our one path to whatever of the big world outside we could ever hope to see. And we planned to take it.

And so, together, we said a bit louder and throwing all our voices into the last note, "Ill-a-Rose-O!" The great ape rustled on his stool, and outside the tent one of the white horses shook its mane. And Jack Burton laughed loudly at us.

"Damned dancing girls," he muttered softly under his breath, thinking we wouldn't hear him, or understand. Then he looked down at both of us, and the sparkle of his eyes held us tight, and he said, "It's not ILL-A-ROSE-O, my boys. My name is Il Rosso," and the "r" tripped of his tongue with a whir and the "s" sound burred and buzzed, as he made this name sound like a song.

"Il Rosso," we imitated the roll and the buzz.

"Il Rosso," he repeated, and it took us a few more tries to get it right, or close to right, to make it sing off our lips like it did from his. But sing it out we did. Again and again.

"Il Rosso."

"What does it mean?" I said, and I settled down in the hard pillow, putting my hands out behind me to rest my back, and without realizing it, feeling more comfortable and at home there on the ground, in our little circle by the heater.

Burton sank back in his chair, as if it was some overstuffed Lazy Boy and not a wheelchair, and he seemed as comfortable as if he was sitting in the lap of some luxurious study within a dark and many roomed Victorian manse, beside a roaring, cozy fire, surrounded by leather bound books and not canvas walls. But he was only resting back on a worn wheelchair, made of steel and some sort of artificial leather vinyl, fraying at the edges into dirty white twine.

"It means the Red," Burton said wistfully. "And if I were to tell it to you whole, boys, it'd be Il Rosso Piccolo. The Little Red Lad." He chuckled a little and looked into Robbie's eyes. "Or Little Red, I guess. That'd catch it." He smiled at us and whispered, "Il Rosso Piccolo."

"Did your hair used to be red?" Robbie asked. He was thinking, I know, of this kid a grade between us in school, Red Gleason, with a shock of hair on his head the color of a peony, because I was thinking of Red Gleason too, and trying to fit him to the old man in the chair before us.

Burton brought a hand up and scruffed at the thick grey and white stubble on top of his head, and laughed. "No, no, it wasn't my hair." Then he was quiet, as if he was thinking about what and how much to tell us. He rolled his chair back toward a little wooden chest on the floor behind Butto Sammy. He switched a tiny tin latch back and flipped the carved lid back on its hinges. From where I sat, if I leaned way over to the side, I could see the soft fabric lining, bright red, inside the little chest, but I couldn't see what was inside it. He pulled some things out of that box, tossed some of them in his lap, and kept the other, smaller items, hidden in one hand, before he slapped the lid of the chest shut.

Then with his one free hand, he wound himself back around toward Robbie and me. Once he was settled again, back in the circle around that little propane heater where we all sat, with that same free hand he picked up by its bowl an ivory pipe with a thin, curved stem as long as my forearm. It was all of one piece, smooth and yellowed a little from handling and age.

"No, my boys," he said. "That name has to do with the shirt that's hanging out there to dry." He pointed with the long yellow-white stem of his pipe toward the canvas walls and the ceiling of the tent. But he meant what we had seen hanging outside, in the cool night air of the summer. Then Burton looked over to the ape. "Butto," he said softly, "mi porta la camicia."

The gorilla looked at him, and then at us with his beady black eyes, as if to be sure it was all right, then he rose from the stool and lumbered gently across the tent, walking on his hind feet and on the knuckles of his front paws. With barely a motion of one of his arms, he slipped smoothly through the tent flap and out into the dark outside.

I thought, 'If only Mrs. Coogan and all of her kind out there in our little bitty town could know that the great, beady eyed ape was free and loose, wandering unfettered and unattended, in the dark knight of their summer dreams, it would shake them all to the root of their safe and secure souls.'

"It was the General who gave me that name," Burton said proudly, "back after our first battle in his own countryside. Back after his great defeat." He was looking at the pipe in his lap, and he seemed far away. "I wasn't always in a chair like this, ragazzi. There was a time when I could run faster than you can dream, and I could climb up into the billowing sails of a ship, higher above the world than you can imagine. There was a time, O ragazzi."

Robbie sat beside his knapsack, entranced. "When was that, sir?" he said, gazing up at Burton in his chair.

"Long ago, I guess," he said wistfully. "Long ago, by your time anyway."

I didn't understand then what he meant, speaking of "our time." Many years would pass, and I would have to do a lot of growing up, and even then I would need to learn to give up on the things that I knew, before I could began to understand the mystery that he meant when he spoke of "our time." Because, for one thing, it was really the mystery that was "his time" that was past any rational understanding. But that night, in that moment, was the beginning of my understanding of the mystery of time, of how it bends and stretches and turns back on itself, and how the age of the hairs on your head has little to do, and everything to do, with the way your memory winds and curls around "your time," always seeming to run relentlessly forward, but never until you finally disappear is it able truly to escape the fronds of the past that lap over into the present and make the future repeat itself over and over again. That night, in that sentence, "Long ago, by your time, anyway," was the beginning of all that for me. And in some real way, more real than that relentless press forward, and more real than the difference between my brother's tallow haired fluff and the brisk, steely gray on Burton's head, that moment when Jack Burton whispered about "my time" to me, that moment still lives, right now, and requires all the searches and questions, all the moments that follow it, seemingly without end, but in the end illusory beside that one moment of that one night "long ago" where this all began. In our time.

"All of my people, my father, my mother, my brothers and sisters, they had all died," Burton said. "And I seemed to be only about your age, Will. When I seemed to be about your age, Will, I had already outlived them all. So I was all alone in Montevideo, working on the docks, doing whatever I could to get on.

"I seemed to be young and spry," Burton whispered, "and I was spry. Yet I had outlived them all. I was young enough still, to need to do the hard work to eat, to feed myself. So I was carrying bales and hauling barrels of pickled beef and crates of cheeses. My back was my only asset, you know. That's when Ciccio found me. You see, he thought I was just a lad."

The door flap of the tent parted and into the yellow lantern light Butto Sam slipped soundlessly. His black eyes glanced at me and at Robbie, not trusting us, then he blew a hard, clicking breath through his teeth, just once, and he lumbered back over to his low wooden stool. The knuckles of his right front paw held his shoulders and head up, as he moved across the floor of the tent, walking three legged.

His left paw was pressed against his chest. And in it he clutched Burton's red shirt, gently in that big black hand.

"Ciccio found me working on the docks in Montevideo, and he felt sorry for me, I guess. Because he strolled up to me and said, 'Il piccolo,' that's what he called me right at the start. 'Come with me,' he said. And he gave me a job; I was his steward, he called it. But I was really his student, you know.

"We set sail on a Sardinian brig called the Bifronte, and I've never seen Montevideo or the mouth of the River Platte, or the shores of Uruguay again." Burton reached over to Butto Sammy and without a word or a command, the ape handed him the red shirt, still damp from the night air. "Zio Ciccio," he said, "to him I looked like I was about your age, my little friend, Will. How old are you, lad?"

"Twelve," I said, stretching it by a year.

Robbie looked at me with outraged surprise, and that made Mr. Burton laugh out loud.

"Yes," Burton said, "I guess I looked to my Zio Ciccio like I was about ten or eleven." Then the old man grinned at me, and it made me shrink down on the pillow.

"Age is not a matter of numbers, ragazzi. Trust me, young Willie; it's not got to do with counting the years. Not at all. And that was where Ciccio was wrong. But he had a big heart, and I won't fault him for that, boys. I won't."

Burton held his shirt in his lap, and it covered the long ivory pipe, hiding it from our sight. "He said to me, many, many times, 'Ho un cuore che troppo sente,'" Burton whispered those singsong words, "In the short time that I knew him, he would always say, 'Mi' piccolo, ho un cuore che troppo sente.' And I guess he was right, too."

Then Burton looked up from the red shirt and into Robbie's confused gaze. "It means," Burton smiled sweetly at my little brother, and at me too, "'I have a heart that feels too much.'"

*　　　　*　　　　*

Burton folded the crimson shirt in his lap so the double row of buttons down its front was squared up with the collar. Then he smoothed the folds in the fabric evenly, to crease it, and he set it, pressed tightly now in a square, on top of that little wooden chest. He patted the shirt with something like affection once he had placed it safely aside there.

"I didn't know when we set sail on the Bifronte where we were headed, boys. The ship slipped out of Montevideo into the Atlantic without a touch of fanfare. There was no one waving farewell to us from the docks. No teary eyes on the shore left behind. No. Not a one. And I had not the slightest idea, lads, what our great goal was. How lofty our destination was, lads. How it would change my whole life. For me, it was just work, and a journey that would steer me away and out of South America, where I'd been stuck for too, too long. I had no home to yearn for then, no country even to work my way home toward, for I belonged to the world then, lads, to the whole big world, O ragazzi. I was a man without a country, wandering from land to land. But I knew deep in my heart I didn't belong to Montevideo any longer.

"And I could see, right from the start, that my new friend Ciccio was just trying to help me. My dear old Zio Ciccio," Burton said, as he picked the ivory pipe up from his lap again. "Do you know what 'Zio' means, little one?" he said to Robbie.

My brother didn't speak, he just shook his head slowly no.

"You Zio is your uncle, lads. And before long, that's what I called him, you see. And that's how I came to feel about him. He was my Zio Ciccio."

Robbie kicked his feet out in front of him, and settled on his side, down with one arm over his knapsack, and he never once looked away from Mr. Burton.

"I didn't know anything about him, then, but Zio Ciccio, he says to me, once the Bifronte had lost sight of land, 'We are on a great voyage, il piccolo. This is the beginning of a great and a true adventure.'

"'Where are we going, my Zio?' I asked him.

"We were standing in the prow of the brig, with the Atlantic casting itself against our keel, and the breeze steady at our backs. 'We are going to a country that doesn't exist,' Zio Ciccio said to me. 'We are going to make a country that needs to exist, to free its many lands from all the priests and all the blue bloods.'

"Now, you must realize, my little friends, I didn't know what in hell he was talking about. He made no sense to me at all. No more than you know what I'm telling you about right now. I was as confused as you little lads are right here, and right now. But already I knew, I would entrust my whole life to my Zio. What cause was his, was mine, lads. For if it was his cause, it had to be true and be grand.

"But it was still a long, slow voyage across the wide Atlantic, more than two months we were at sea, always heading to the north and the east, and on the voyage my Ciccio taught me many, many things. Sometimes with tears welling in his eyes, he told me about the Austrian soldiers who ran roughshod over Lombardia and the Veneto, they drank the wine and sang loudly in German in the cafes right down in Piazza San Marco. And he talked of the Frenchmen too, in cahoots with the Popes, those Frenchmen who ruled in Piedmont and the Romagna and propped up the Papal States, with little Napoleons who weren't worthy of that great name. Sometimes he would bemoan the sweet orchards filled with blood oranges on the sides of Mount Etna, and the sweet lemons of Sorrento, all harvested for some Spanish King who reigned in Napoli. 'We are on a voyage to give birth to a country, il piccolo,' Ciccio would say to me, his chest swelling with his dreams. 'We will be the fathers, all of us together, the fathers we need to bring this struggling infant to life, free of the chains of the old Papal Swiss Guards, at last on her own two feet. Standing up, free and straight. Italia. Our Italia!'

"But I didn't understand any of that back then. I just knew this good man, with the fire of dreams in his eyes, he had picked me up from the dirt and the wage slavery of an endless Uruguayan dock, and shared with me his hopes."

Burton paused there to press a pinch of something into the bowl of his long pipe, and then he packed it down hard with his thumb, until it was deep in the bowl. The long ivory stem trembled a bit at the pressure he used in the bowl resting in his palm.

"The first night out, once the shores of Uruguay and Brazil had sunk behind us on the horizon, and the round Brazilian sun sank down chasing after them into the sea, the word went out around the ship. Tonight, at moonrise, we must all meet on deck. Amidships, the General will speak to us. 'Il Generale,' went out the word, from man to man, 'Stasera. Tonight.'"

Burton lifted the pipe to his lips, held it there unlit for a moment, calmly remembering something about that night long ago. Then he took the pipe out of his mouth and gently sniffed at the bowl, to be sure something was right. With his thumb he tamped down again on the paste he'd placed inside the bowl, making sure it was pressed into the tiny bowl even tighter still.

"Zio Ciccio's eyes glowed when he told me, lads, 'Tonight, il piccolo, you will begin to understand. You are going to hear the General speak. Il Generale! Stasera!' We went up onto the deck, gathering amidships, and my Zio sat at the foot of the stairs that lead down from the compass bridge, and I stood next to him. Before long a thin needle of moon began to rise out of the Atlantic off to our starboard, slowly ascending into the star-filled skies. The wind was low and gentle, and the gaffs drooping low in the mizzenmast flapped loosely as the breeze dropped. Ciccio rested his back against the stair and he scrubbed nervously at his clean-shaven chin. His hair was dark black, and he cut it off himself well above his collar, to keep himself cool. He had a black moustache drooping at the corners of his lips, and it was thicker than mine, ragazzi. Thicker than mine is now, as many, many years as these whiskers here have seen, his were thicker still. But Zio Ciccio always kept his chin smooth and clean. I never saw him needing to shave, not once in all that voyage, all those days. Always clean-shaven. Never, I guess, except..." Burton trailed off there, lost in his memories for a moment. The great ape behind him was still, sitting quietly on his stool, listening to the music of Burton's voice, waiting for it to return in the circus night. Butto Sammy's little eyes darted quickly around the room, every now and then, as if he were a guard on the look out, watching for the slightest movement from anyone foolish enough to intrude.

I thought Robbie might be falling asleep, slung out on the Persian rug as he was, with his head resting on one hand propped up by that knapsack of his. But I leaned forward a little so I could see his face, and though he glanced at me with a bit of annoyance, his eyes were wide and locked on Burton.

"Ciccio rested back against the stair," Burton said, still fiddling with the pipe in his lap. "But he seemed weak then, suddenly. His eyes were darker and shadowed by something deep, and he closed them. My Zio coughed a little then, like he had the old remnants of a cold in his chest. He seemed tired suddenly, and I tell you truly I wasn't sure what I should do." Burton reached a hand over absently to touch that red shirt on the little chest, and the ape's eyes followed it all carefully.

"But then there was a stir among all the men on the deck, the fifty or sixty of us in all, everyone crowding out onto the decks between the two masts of the brig. And Ciccio, at the sound of the men's restlessness, he opened his deep eyes and immediately, without glancing around him at all, he rose gracefully up on his feet, as if he'd never coughed and never been weary in all his life.

"And then, ragazzi, the General came up from below. You know, my boys, I'd seen him before, on the docks as we prepared to depart, ordering the supplies stored safely away, laughing and joking with the sailors and the longshoremen all along the docks, like another seaman with his legs tired of walking on the solid ground. But that night, beneath that slivered Brazilian moon, my boys, he came up from below decks and he was different, lads, he was transformed.

"You see, the General, he was not a big man. He stood much shorter than me, by an inch or two, and I'm shy of six feet by some inches, I am. But he was thick and solid and he could stand his ground and you knew he was there, that his boots were filled with iron, you knew that. But this night, O ragazzi, with that needle of a moon low to the starboard and by the light of a million stars to the larboard, the General strode up onto the deck, with an old brown woolen poncho wrapped over his shoulders, draping down over his back like a short, dark cape, and he seemed a foot taller than everyone on board right then. His step up out of the belly of the ship, where he'd been sleeping and eating with all the men, just another human soul down below with the crew, it was that step alone that made a giant of him. Seemed he was no longer one of us, lads. I tell you. He was now Il Generale!"

Burton stopped then and a smile creased one side of his mouth, filled with a pride of having been there at that moment, of having known him on that night, I suppose. His pause didn't last long.

"At the edge of the stair he came upon my Zio, and he stopped. A broad grin broke across his face, and his teeth shone in that smile. He wore a little brown cap, like the peasants of Uruguay and Argentina wear, and though he had it tilted a little over his right eye, he still looked at that moment like some long lost gaucho finding at last the endless grass of the pampas.

"'Il Colonnello!' he said to Ciccio, and my Zio responded with a straight up stance and a salute.

"'My General,' Ciccio said.

"That made the grin on the General's face turn into a gentle laugh. He clapped my Zio on the shoulder and said, 'Ciccio, tonight we begin our journey home at last, my friend. Our journey, Ciccio, to make our home.'

"A big smile opened on my Zio's face, and his eyes glowed again like they did when he asked me to come along on this voyage. He laughed too, just a bit, but with an irrepressible excitement. 'At last, Peppino,' he said. 'At last.'

"Then he turned his brown eyes on me. 'And who is this young man, Il Colonnello?' The General had fair, but not blonde hair. There was a bit of red to it like the light mane on a chestnut mare. It was growing long and it hung down to touch his collar, and he had a full beard and moustache of the same fair color. His beard was so thick it seemed to grow straight out from his cheeks. His eyes looked me up and down, measuring me, and they were the lightest brown I've ever seen of a pair of eyes, and they were sweet and soft, but piercing too. They gazed right through my soul and read me inside and out like a newspaper headline, in bold print, and all of that in just a moment of time, and yet there was no level of judgment in them. They just looked into my very being, and accepted what was there to be seen. And after a moment of that, I swore to myself I would follow this man anywhere he asked me to go.

"'This is Gianni, my nipote,' Ciccio said, and I hate to admit it, my lads, but I blushed as red as a virgin babe on her wedding night. See, he called me his nephew, lads, his 'nipote.' I had no idea he felt that way about me. You know, I called him Zio, and I sure saw him in so short a time as the only family I had in the world. But I had no idea my caro Ciccio would call me his blood. And to the General, too. But there it was, ragazzi. He says to the General himself, while I'm all tongue tied and dumbfounded, 'Peppino, this is my nipote.'"

Robbie pulled his legs in and sat up straight, Indian style by his knapsack, and I realized that I was leaning forward toward him and Burton too. I think now we were both nodding our heads yes, we knew the feeling, in so short a time. To be family, or maybe something even stronger than that, when kindred souls meet on the wandering roads of the big wide world. Robbie and I, we knew what he meant. We knew that night. And we believed.

"'Peppino,' he said to the General as he reached out a hand and put it on my shoulder. "This young boy has the heart of a free man. He will help us to make our home, Peppino.'

"Then Il Generale stared deep into my eyes, and locked my soul into place with his fair brown stare, and it was a moment of time that seemed to stretch out over the years, ragazzi. I can feel it even now, as I try to tell you this story."

Jack Burton's own gaze fixed on something past the walls of the tent and out into the grassy schoolyard beyond, and he seemed lost in this distant past as he spoke.

"It's hard to describe a moment like that," he said, and his stare hardened as the corners of his eyes creased into loud crow's feet. "It's a moment, my little friends, when there are no calendars or clocks. It is part of the always now, you see. It will never go away from me, not as long as I breathe." He stopped there, and then he gazed at me, and I felt his eyes bore down inside of me with a magnetism I'd never felt before.

"That moment, when the General gazed into my soul," Burton whispered now as if he wasn't even speaking to us, "it is more real to me than this moment right now, and it glows in a hard true light, deep down in my soul, lads, deep down into the cellars of my soul."

Butto Sammy stirred on his stool, and I swear there was some sort of flash of light or something, but I heard Burton say, "That moment. It will never die."

Robbie and I had never heard anyone speak like that, especially an adult as incandescent as Burton was just then. Even at our grandmother's funeral, where there were tears and wailing that we barely understood, and there were lots of fervent prayers in the pews, and sacred words read from the pulpit. We had never heard anyone, child or man, speak with such intensity. Burton looked away, and then he held up that ivory pipe of his, and pressed his thumb down in the bowl again, but it was still unlit, and then he spoke.

"'I think you may be right,' the General said to my Zio. And then Il Generale asked me my name, and I answered him, and it was as if from that moment on I had enlisted in our cause. By just speaking my name out loud, I had signed on, though I didn't even know then what our direction would be."

Burton sat back in his wheelchair, and I realized at that moment that it wasn't just we boys who'd been stretching toward him as he spoke. He had been leaning out of his chair toward us. "Butto," he said. "Fuoco, Butto."

The ape rose from its stool and took out a heavy steel urn, the size of my palm, from inside that strange little box, being careful not to drop or wrinkle the red shirt that sat on top of it. He held the urn over to Mr. Burton, and the old man cradled it in his hand, his two first fingers on one side of the steel urn's stem, his last two fingers on the other side. With his thumb he flicked the lid of the urn back and revealed that the thing was some sort of elaborate lighter. With his thumb then he worked the lighter and the low yellow and blue flame sprang to life.

He put the long-stemmed pipe in his mouth with the bowl tilted sideways and he laid the flame up against the bowl, and drew in a long swallow of breath. Almost no smoke escaped from the pipe, it all went into his lungs, and then he breathed it out. It was strange, like no smoke I'd ever smelled before, as acrid and sweet as church incense, but not so heavy in the air. I found myself breathing deep, trying to absorb the scent of it all around me.

Before he rested back in the wheelchair, he turned the long stem of his pipe over to Butto Sammy. The ape took the ivory stem into his black lips. Burton tilted the flame into the bowl again and the mountain gorilla drew it in without any coaching.

Then Burton handed the pipe and the urn lighter back to Butto Sammy, and he rested down in the chair for a long moment, his eyes staring blankly down into his lamp.

61

Robbie looked over at me, with a million questions in his eyes, but I just shrugged. So Robbie asked, "What did the General do then?"

It roused the old man from his reverie and made him laugh. He whispered his name, quietly, to himself really. "Il Rosso," he whispered. Then he looked from Robbie to me and back again. "Ah, yes," he said, "my Ciccio, he was telling the General who I was. 'He is a good lad, Peppino,' my Zio said, while the General was staring me in the eyes." At that point, Burton held first my eyes and then Robbie's in his stare, but without stopping his tale. " And the General, after he's looked me over, he said to Ciccio, 'He will do,' with a little note of approval. He reached out and touched my shoulder, right where Ciccio still had his hand on my shoulder, remember, lads. And then he said again, 'He will do.'"

While Burton spoke, the ape took a little spoon and gently scoured the inside of the bowl of the ivory pipe with it, cleaning out all of the burnt black crust. Butto Sammy was swift and skillful, working with the little spoon in his big paw, completely engrossed in his chore.

"The General walked away from us then, leaving with just a little, casual salute to Ciccio and a muttered, 'Il Colonello.' The he strode out to amidships, among the 50 or so men of the Legion, and stood on his sure sea legs as he slowly strolled around among them, touching a hand here or a shoulder there, greeting others with a grin or a laugh or a quiet, private word you couldn't catch. A name, a title, a rank. We were all waiting for him to speak."

The ape took that little spoon, with its accumulated crust, and put it in his mouth, licking it clean. Then he, almost silently, opened up the little box under the red shirt, and into it the pipe and the urn and the spoon all disappeared. Without noticing a thing, Burton just went on with his story.

"That old Sardinian brig rocked gently in the South Atlantic sea," he said, "and the General paused there. He put his hands behind his back, they were hidden under his poncho, and he strolled slowly across the decks. The men parted around him, though we were all crowded into the same space. And there was whispering and excited muttering all around. Now and then a few agitated laughs would rise from one corner or another, from that little group of friends, or from those two or three men here and there. But the General, he just strolled thoughtfully across the deck, his head lowered a bit as he seemed to ponder how to tell us of the hard dangers that lay ahead. The brown of his poncho flapped a little, as it brushed against the men on deck. When he strode over beneath the mainmast, he turned back, and he lifted his head so his fair beard pointed out high and proud. The evening breeze caught at the fair locks of his hair around his collar, lifted them in a ripple, and then again.

"'We are headed home, mi' amici,' he said. But you know, lads, all his words are gone from me. I can see him, standing in that evening breeze, his voice booming out to us, his hands outstretched to us, and then from time to time he would pound a fist into his palm to make his point clear. I don't think, either, that he spoke for long, lads, though to me now, remembering it all this very night, he seemed to speak forever. But the words, O ragazzi, they are gone. I can remember almost none of them, only these few that I report to you now tonight, and that's it. He began by saying to us all, 'We are headed home, my friends.' And then there was the one word that rang out often, through all of what he said. I remember that, because he seemed to repeat it like it was

the refrain to his song. Freedom! He would say. 'Liberta'!'
It would ring and ring in all our ears. Liberta'!

"And each time it set loose a great huzzah from all the
men. I looked over at my Ciccio, and though the shadows
still covered his eyes, he held a fist in the air above his head,
and a broad smile filled his cheeks, and he shouted,
'Liberta'! Liberta'!' This was what he loved the most.
'Liberta'!'

Burton's own hand had closed into a fist and he held
it up in the air as high as his head, as if he was grasping at
something in the air, and he grinned at us. "Liberta'!" he
said. "Liberta'!"

And Robbie and I joined in, each time, in an echo.
"Liberta'!" we yelled, and while I was grinning, Robbie
looked back at me with a fire in his eyes that had nothing to
do with just having fun, and everything to do with his
freedom. You see, for me it was just a rebel yell, a cowboy
shout, and tomorrow I could change sides and be the Indian.
But for Robbie, the oppression of being grounded in his
room, the grand injustice of being punished just for trying to
see a gorilla, it filled him with a real desire to break free.
"Liberta'!" he yelled, from deep in his little heart, and with
his knapsack cradled under his arm, he was I know ready to
follow Jack Burton anywhere.

After a moment, Jack Burton went on quietly, "What
a night that was, ragazzi, on the quiet, cool sea, under the
sliver of a southern moon, Il Generale pulling us all
together, speaking from deep in his soul, until we all became
one lone heart, beating strong, beating together. And while
he spoke, , a tall black man dressed in a scarlet blouse
moved across the deck toward Ciccio and me. He smiled at
us and stood very close to my Zio. 'Buona sera, il
Colonello,' he said, and then he nodded at me, too, because
I was so clearly close at hand.

"'Liberta', Aguiar!' Ciccio answered him softly, grinning."

Burton looked over at me, and suddenly felt the need to explain. "This was the great Aguiar, my little friends. Aguiar, the General's batman, by his side in all the struggles from Gualeguay and Rio Grande do Sul to San Antonio, and in the expedition to Salto, too. Aguiar was there, and he was with us across the lakes and on into the Swiss frontier. Still he rode next to the General, on his midnight black steed, sporting the scarlet of Montevideo, until finally he fell that summer's day, defending the fallen Roman Republic. Aguiar, miei ragazzi. Next to my Zio, I think, he was the closest comrade the General had. In those days."

Burton paused a moment, seeing both these men in his mind's eye I suppose, and then realizing too that Robbie and I were now confused. "But I'm getting ahead of myself, boys," he said. "These are things still to come in the swirling clouds of time."

Jack Burton sat quietly then for a moment, resting his eyes and he seemed to relax and slowly gather his senses together. When the euphoria of the smoke mixed with memories cleared from his mind, he seemed ready to go on. "It was after the General was done and we all of us knew that we would follow him and defend him and our freedom, right to the Gates of Hell herself, it was then he gave his orders, softly, though his voice grew a little louder and firmer as he went on. 'During this voyage,' he said, 'those of you who know how to read and write will be teaching those of you who are now ready to learn. And that, my compatriots,' the General paused to clip us to attention, 'that would be any of you who can't read.'"

Robbie looked back over at me, confused again, and I was too. I mean, I thought, what's the big holy deal about reading and writing? But then I noticed Robbie's eyes were big with some kind of fear, and not just this confusion of mine.

Burton saw the looks on our confused little faces, and he went on, " I remember the General folded his arms over his chest, and announced, 'So now, who here is ready to learn? Raise your hands.' It was not a question, lads. No, little friends, it was an order.

"And, O ragazzi miei, I was one of them. In all my years, scrounging and scruffing along, I'd never once seen the inside of a schoolroom. Not once. I'd never cracked open a book or read a paper. And I was ashamed, because by God I could scale the rigging like a spider, and I could even take the wheel and steer the whole damn ship, and I could follow a compass and even name the stars in all the Southern skies, and I knew the planets by name when they rose in the heavens. But I couldn't even read my own name, boys. I signed 'John Burton' only when I had to, and when I did, I had to use an 'X,' lads. Just an X.

"And so, with more fear than if the brig was plunging into heavy seas and taking on water, I raised my hand in front of the General. Aguiar had an arm around my Ciccio's shoulder now, and Ciccio said quietly, 'I will teach you.' And I looked at my Zio and his tall friend, both of them so close to the Generale, standing side by side, then all my fears faded away like so much fog under the morning sun. That's all he said, ragazzi. No big words or plans, he just said, 'I will teach you.' And over the next few months, he did."

"You mean," Robbie blurted out, "you had to go to school?"

Mr. Burton looked up at my little brother, and I saw the slight haze of the sweet smoke from his pipe behind the color in his eyes. He smiled very gently and then he nodded his head yes.

"Ahhh, Geez," Robbie moaned, but Burton raised an open hand, just the way the General had done in the story he told us, and Robbie sunk down on his knapsack, and didn't make another sound.

"That night, my little friends, the General did one last thing. He strode from beneath that mainmast to amidships, and the men all stood and moved closer around him, as if by instinct. My Zio stood tall as he could and stepped into the circle gathering around the General. I followed behind him, and Aquiar once again slid easily through the crowd until he stood, solid on both feet, right beside my dear Ciccio.

"The General looked all around at us, turning in a circle so he could look each of us in the eye, one by one, slowly. And as he turned, arms now crossed on his chest, he asked us, one by one it almost seemed, 'What is the name of this ship?' And we answered 'Bifronte,' and some said, 'The brig Bifronte,' or sang out, 'Bifronte, flying the colors of Sardinia.'

"'This is no longer a suitable name for a ship bearing so much of the future in her hold. No, my friends, she is no longer the Bifronte. Not on this voyage, she is not.'

"Then the General reached over to his friend and batman Aguiar, standing close beside my Ciccio. And Aguiar, from inside his red blouse, pulled out a bottle of brandy, taken from the stores below. It had all been carefully planned. Aguiar handed the bottle over and the General held it in both his hands, and then he seemed to speak it, 'Bifronte is not a name for the bark of grand venture. No, my compatriots.'

"Then the General strode out of our circle, past the backstay and the shroud, and around the foremast until he had climbed out into the bow of the ship. He stepped up and put a foot on the bowsprit and raised that bottle up to that Brazilian moon and the southern stars. Everyone crowded into the bow after him.

"'Good brig Bifronte,' the Generale announced to the sea and the stars, 'We, the Italian Legion of Montevideo, the Victors of the Pampas sailing home to our freedom, we christen thee . . . ' and he paused there and took that brandy and crashed the bottle into the bowsprit, 'La Speranza.' And a great yell rose up from all of us. 'La Speranza,' we yelled in one voice. 'La Speranza.'

"From out of nowhere, but certainly from somewhere Aguiar had carefully prepared, two open bottles of brandy appeared. And they went from hand to hand, and that name became a toast, over and over, 'Speranza,' we cried. 'Speranza,' we whispered. The hard wine tasted bitter and strong, always chasing down that name, 'Speranza.'"

Burton leaned forward in his wheelchair, and he took little Robbie's shoulder in his hand, and his other hand reached out across the tent toward me. In his eyes was the fire that lay behind whatever it was he'd been smoking, but it echoed the taste of that brandy from years before. "Speranza," he whispered to us.

Butto Sammy stirred on his stool at the sound of that word, at the urgency in the old man's voice. "Speranza," Burton whispered again.

Robbie and I sat frozen and still, while he sat back in his chair then and tilted his head back and laughed long and hard, with a deep happiness that made you hungry to share in it with him. "'Speranza,' my General cried," Burton nodded.

"Speranza," Robbie whispered, rising a little from the knapsack. And so I joined in too.

"Speranza," we said together, in hushed, little boy tones.

And then everything was silent for a while. Burton seemed content, resting there in his thoughts and the great ape sat quietly on his stool, gazing fondly at the old man. Something of the same soft glow that shone in Burton's look sang behind his grey black eyes. The sweet vanished smoke of contentment.

For a while only the choruses of summer crickets made any sound, and then as if to start us out of some reverie, an owl who-hooted once in the night.

"What does it mean, sir?" Robbie spouted up.

Burton smiled fondly at my little brother. He stayed, resting back in his wheelchair, not sitting up or moving a limb. He just said, "Hope, il piccolo. It means Hope."

"La Speranza," said Robbie again.

Burton took a deep breath and he scrubbed his hand across his chin. It was hard to tell if it was memories or smoke that drifted through his mind just then. But suddenly he went on with his story. "It was the next morning I dug out this Bible of mine. Some missionary in the backwaters of Argentina had forced it on my father, when my old man was dying of hard, strange fevers in Costa Brava, up the river from Montevideo. This was the book, the only one I had, that I took to Ciccio and said to him, 'Teach me to read, caro Zio.'

"Ciccio took the volume out of my hands and turned it over once or twice, looking at its cheap cardboard binding. 'Where did you get this?' he asked.

"I told him the book's story, and he seemed to look at it differently then. Just when I thought he might throw it overboard, he handed it back to me, and then he reached inside his shirt and pulled out some loose, blank sheets of paper.

"'I'll teach you to read, il piccolo, but not with that,' he said. 'Enough evil has been done in this world with those words. You don't need to start reading with that.'

"Then he wrote out the letters of the alphabet, one at a time. And after them five words. And so we began. We practiced every letter and its sound. And then we did it again.

"Then he pointed at the first word on the paper, with his finger leading me along, pointing back to the rows of alphabet from time to time, prompting me when I need it, he helped me to read my first word. 'Jack,' I read aloud, and then 'Jack Burton.' See, Ciccio showed me how the sounds and the letters worked until I could read my own name. And that was where we started. 'Later on, when you can read on your own, il piccolo, then you can read that Bible of your father's if you want. But you must start first with your own name. That will set you free.' And Ciccio nodded sternly at that thought."

Burton ran a tongue around his teeth and sighed deeply, and sat for a moment. "Cibo, Butto?" he softly asked the ape. Butto Sammy looked up from his own reverie, and stared calmly at the man in the wheelchair. "Cibo?" Burton repeated, even more quietly.

And so, with a soft, clacking snort, Butto Sammy slid forward off his stool and put part of his weight onto his knuckles, and out of the tent he lumbered, into the cricket filled night.

"What were the other three words?" I asked.

"Yeah!" Robbie piped up.

Burton grinned, and he hid his smile under the finger that he brushed at his moustache with. "So you were listening, lads. You were. Even if I was telling you about 'my schooling' on board that ship."

Outside we heard one of the doors to the Buick open with a creak. Butto Sammy was climbing into the car.

"What were the other three words?" I asked again.

"Ah, the next two were tough, my boys. I couldn't get them that first day, and it took me a couple of days to read them easily. And my Zio, he had to break them up into parts, so I could read the words piece by piece. But they were Ciccio's name. That's what they were. 'Francesco Anzani.'"

He let the name roll off his tongue like music, and he seemed to think we would know it, recognize the name of this great "Colonnello." But of course we didn't. "'Francesco Anzani,'" Burton repeated, for sheer love of the sound, and maybe for love of the name too. Then he looked at us, through his hazy eyes, and said, "It's a name the whole world should know by heart. My dear Ciccio. But he's been forgotten, 'lo these many years. We only remember Il Generale, only his name resounds through all the seasons, not 'Aguiar' who stood with him, and not my Zio, 'Francesco Anzani.' They are forgotten."

Suddenly Burton shot up in his chair, leaning out to where he could grab Robbie by the shoulder. There was a crazy fire in his eyes that belied the many things he had done and might do in the world. "But not by me, santo cielo! Not by me. I'll carry those names down through time, forever and ever."

It seemed that he should have added, "until the day I die" to the end of that "forever and ever," but he didn't. Not then and not ever. And this is why I still search for traces of him, everywhere I go.

*   *   *

"What was the last word?" said Robbie, as if the fire inside Jack Burton had spread into him through the grasp of the old man's hand.

Burton held his shoulder in his grasp, and he looked at him, and then at me. "Il piccolo, bring me that desk, mi' figlio. Over there." He pointed to a wooden chest in the far corner of the tent, sitting on a set of wheels.

Robbie hopped up and nearly skipped over to the trunk, he was so full of the energy of discovery. "Inside there," he said. The chest was about half the size of a steamer trunk, made of wood that was grayed with age and worn by handling at the edges of the lid. The hinges were brass and the corners had brass tips. But the wood was old and its finish had worn mostly off. Big straps of black fraying leather stapled with brass tacks to the wood held it latched.

"Open it up and, bring me my desk, my boy," Burton said.

I rose up onto my knees, because I wanted to see what was down inside the chest, even if I hadn't been the one chosen for the chore.

"Yes, sir, Mister," said Robbie, restraining a giggle of delight.

Robbie flipped back the soft latches and opened up the case. Inside it were stacks of paper, filled with handwriting and carefully bundled together with string. Off to one side rested a dark wooden lap desk.

"There, bring me that, my boy," Burton said.

Robbie lifted the lap desk out of the chest and brought it over to Burton, who took it and set it gently on his knees. It was obvious from the way that the desk rested comfortably in his lap that he had held it there for many hours on many a night.

Burton opened the lid of the little desk and extracted from it a plain white piece of paper, a pair of glasses and a large wine-colored pen. Then he carefully closed the lid and, setting the paper securely on the desk, and the wire-rimmed glasses on his nose, he wrote out some words with the deep indigo ink of his fountain pen.

While Burton wrote, Robbie closed the lid of the little trunk and slipped back beside his knapsack, which I think he now saw as his little trunk of valuables, someday to be filled with treasures just like these things in the old wooden chests of Jack Burton.

Outside there was a squeak from the car door, and then we heard it slam closed latched softly. In a moment, that tent flap parted and in waddled Butto Sammy, one of his arms cradling a bottle and a wrinkled brown paper sack, the other arm working as his third leg. "Ah, grazie, Butto, grazie," Burton said quietly, without looking up from his desk. Butto set the bottle and the sack on the rug beside Burton, and then went straight back to his stool, though his attention was locked onto the things he'd carried in.

A moment passed, and Burton was done. He handed us the sheet of paper. Robbie and I held it between us, each with a hand on the paper, like it was some sort of relic. "This is how I learned to read, my boys. From a sheet of paper that looked just like that one."

Burton's handwriting was large and florid with lots of tales and feathers, and over the years as I have pursued him through many times and places, I have come to know that handwriting well, from the traces and fragments he has left behind him, and at least once in an anonymous manuscript. I knew it was his by that very hand, not to mention the abandoned diary found in Siracusa that I still believe was his, though no one else (including Robbie) will agree, and the two or three times he had left me a letter or a note, before he slipped away again to unknown parts. But that night I was looking at his hand for the first time, and I couldn't help but see how ornate and decorated it was, while still always remaining absolutely clear.

Robbie was staring at the sheet of paper, trying not just to read it but to see into its deeper truth. While we read, Burton picked up the bottle and uncorked it. It had been opened before, and the cork had been shoved back into it, so it slipped out into Burton's hand with barely a pop.

The words and letters on the page were odd, not what I expected to see. But it took a few moments to understand what was missing. Robbie noticed the name first, and then, at the moment he spoke, I saw what was missing in the alphabet.

"Hey, Mr. Burton," Robbie said, his nose scrunched up around his glassed, "that's not your name, sir."

Burton had extracted a flat chunk of ham and a ball of hard white cheese from his paper sack. Then Butto Sammy, without any command, drew a little knife out of somewhere, and handed it to Burton.

I counted them over, and saw there was only 21 letters to his alphabet, written carefully across the top of the page in three downward columns.

"Where's your name on here?" Robbie demanded.

Burton took the little palm knife from the ape and he draped a white cloth over the lap desk. He straightened it carefully so it covered all the wood, and then he set the ball of white cheese on it alongside the flat ham.

There were several letters missing from his alphabet, and I quietly began to figure out what was left out. Because the large capital letters were arranged in columns, it took a while to see them, and I noticed the gap at the end first. There was no 'w,' 'x,' or 'y' on this sheet.

"What's this 'Gig Anna'?" Robbie said.

Burton chuckled a little, and silently proceeded to pare slices from the ham. Once he had a little stack of the salted meat, he took up the ball of cheese and curling it around in his palm, he deftly shaved long yellow-white spirals from it. There was a look on his face, as he gazed through the glasses on the end of his nose, of great and simple contentment.

And I saw next, by starting at the beginning, that there was no 'j' or 'k' in his alphabet, either. All the rest of the letters appeared to be on the paper, though. I didn't say anything about the strange, short alphabet, as yet.

"That's my name, il piccolo," Burton said, not looking up, paring out his spirals of cheese, each one a little longer and a little more curled than the last.

"'Gig,'" said Robbie, "'Anny,'" more than a little outraged.

Suddenly it clicked. For some reason there was no 'j' or 'k' in his alphabet, and that made it pretty tough to write out 'Jack' on a piece of paper. Or even the more formal 'John' for that matter.

"That is his name," I said, proud of myself. "See," I pointed at the first set of letters. "This says 'Johnny Burtoni,' doesn't it?"

Mr. Burton looked up from his preparations, over his spectacles, and smiled at me, "Very good, mi' ragazzo. Bravo."

"Gianni Burtoni," I repeated, reading the letters that he'd written in his flashy hand.

"But why is it spelled like that?" Robbie protested.

"Because, il piccolo, it's not written in English," Burton said. "English may be my first language, and when I met my Zio we were speaking Spanish, you know, but, il piccolo, he taught me to read in his language, in Italiano. Because this is where we were headed on the Speranza."

"'Gianni Burtoni,'" Robbie read from the page.

Burton chuckled, and muttered, "Very good, little one."

"And this is Francesco Anzani," I read out, torturing the pronunciation.

"Si," Burton said, "my Zio," and then he let the name roll from his lips with all its music, softening the first 'c' into an Italian 'ch.' "Francesco Anzani." he said. He set the knife down on his little lap table, and rested back in his chair from a moment, gazing again at something in the haze of smoke and memory.

"Francesco Anzani," I repeated.

Then Robbie read out the last word on the page, or at least his version of it. "Liberty!" he exclaimed.

Burton let a little smile drift across his lips, and then he said through the haze behind his eyes, "Liberta'."

"Liberta'," I repeated in my best faux Italian, pointing for my little brother at the last letter on the word.

Then Robbie and I read it out together. "Liberta'."

At that point, Jack Burton surprised me again, as he has always and continually seemed to do everywhere and everytime I have found him, or even any trace of him. He carefully selected a slice of the ham and a curl of the cheese and he handed them over to Butto Sammy. He who brought the food always ate first, in the circle of Jack Burton. "Cibo, Sammy," he said, and the food disappeared into the ape's big paws and then it was gone.

Burton took a long swallow from the wine bottle, relishing its taste, and then he offered us the food by holding out his lap desk, turned now into a serving tray. Butto Sammy watched the tray as it was held out toward us, but never moved for it, and every few moments Burton world handed him another sliver of ham and another curl of the hard cheese.

"So a paper just like that one was how I started to read," Burton continued, as we munched on the food. "Everyday, my Zio would write out more and before long he had me reading sentences and writing them out on my own.   Soon, what he wrote out were questions, and I would have to answer them on the paper, with his help."

The meat and cheese were salty and bitter, not really the kind of food that Robbie or I would eat, if we were home and having lunch at the table. It was the kind of stuff that Robbie would complain and whine about, and leave little crumbled up and fingered chunks of on his plate. But we both took it up eagerly now, and we chewed hardily on the provisions. For me, it was curiosity about what this man and his ape lived on, and a deep sense of adventure. Robbie was the really picky eater, at home he was always moving his food around and around the plate, seeming to hope it would either change or go away. But there was none of that here. Robbie had plans to ride off over the horizon with this traveling troupe, and if this is what Jack Burton ate as he rolled merrily along, then even Robbie was going to do his best, and clean his plate without a word.

"After a while, I graduated up to some pages of old newspapers that were left on board the brig," Burton said. "They were mostly old news from Sardinia, about the King and all his doings, and Ciccio would always comment on them, editorializing on what was left out between all the words and the headlines. It usually had to do, my Zio's comments, with peasants doing all the work while the aristocrat lived off the wealth of the countryside and the fruits of the common man's labor.

"'The time has come to turn this over,' Ciccio would say, and his gaze would wander over my head and past the sails into the blue Atlantic heavens, my boys.   His gaze

would stare at the horizon. 'The time has come,' he'd say."
Burton stopped there, and ate a little of his food quietly, but
a great sadness seemed to radiate from him then and linger
low on the tent.

"It was around that time," he said, after a long while
and after another swallow or two of wine, "I began to notice
how, late in the day, when Ciccio would be teaching me to
read, before the dark of night came on, that his hand would
tremble. He would be handing me a piece of old newspaper,
and suddenly the whole paper would shake, just a little, and
only for a moment, but it was a definite shake.

"'Growing chilly in the night air, non e' vero?' he
would say, and laugh, and though it was still warm on the
deck, he'd pull a piece of blanket around him, before we'd
continue. But then, latter on, he would be pointing with his
finger to a word I couldn't make out, and he'd slow me
down and make me pronounce every letter until I could get
it right. But in the middle of this, his finger would tremble,
and quickly he'd withdraw his hand.

"'Ciccio, are you all right?' I would say.

"'It's just the cool air out here,' he'd answer me. But
sometimes, as the voyage lingered on, it would happen
when we were below decks. And then, I wouldn't say
anything, and Ciccio would just ask me a question about
another word, or give a little speech about the peasants and
the lords, or just plain hurry on to something else."

"Was he sick?" Robbie asked.

Burton looked fondly over at Robbie, and then over at
me, and then he said, "In the daylight, Ciccio and Aguiar
and I, we would take our shift, and all three of us could hoist
sails and run the rigging and move our stores in the hold
around, we'd work hard and sweat would pour from us like
a spring. And I seemed to get stronger and more fit as the
voyage went on, just the way the General wanted. Aguiar
was already a mountain of muscle and strength, and the

three of us together, I felt like we could do anything that was asked of us. And I still believe we could.

"See, Francesco, my Zio, was a little man, but not slight. He had arms that were thick with muscle, and they seemed, like his square chest, to be trying to rip out of any shirt he wore. Even out of the crimson blouse of the Italian Legion.

"But I just noticed it, in the evenings, when he would teach me to read, that sometimes he would tremble. He was no youngster, you know, he was a full-grown man, but I began to see the gray strands of hair on his temples and running through the droopy moustache he wore. Every day I thought I could see more and more of them."

Then Burton spoke in a long sigh, gazing somewhere past us into the thin air, "I'd already outlived everyone who loved me, all of them, every one. So I guess that's why I couldn't see it, boys. Because I didn't want to see it coming at me again, and so I tell you I didn't." He paused again and took a long draught from the bottle, and then he gave a healthy handful of slivered meat to Zambutti Sam, while he whispered something softly in Italian to the ape, and one of his hands stroked the ape's head like he was a puppy. "I tell you, I didn't see it," he muttered to no one, and to everyone at once.

Without looking back at us, he went on, "Then came the night of the storm. It had been a peaceful voyage thus far, but that night I was below decks with Ciccio. The seas were a little rough, and so the night's reading lesson was hard. Ciccio turned in, and I noticed that his eyes seemed even darker in the shadows than usual. I sat up in an upper bunk and tried to write in a little journal my Ciccio had given me, but the ship began to rock too much to write and then even to read, so before long I fell asleep too.

"Aguiar was on the first watch that night, and I believe I can say we stayed alive because it was him. Somewhere in the dark of that night, the head of that storm hit us and the seas rose up like open jaws and swept over the decks, and the little brig started to pitch to and fro, and the waves threw us around like a paper boat. But it was the yell of Aguiar that roused me. I heard his big, bass voice call out, 'Fire on board! Fire!'"

Burton lifted his hand up to his tensed shoulders, and his eyes were wide. "I sat up straight in the bunk, 'Fire,' I thought." He leaned back in his chair and his eyes were wild now. "My God, boys. 'Fire on board!' I tell you, ragazzi, there is nothing in the world as frightening as that alarm in the night. To be far out at sea, with nothing but the broad ocean all around you as far as anyone can see, and to be tossing about and fighting to stay afloat in the high waters, in a wooden boat, ragazzi, a ship made of wood from stem to stern, and then to hear those words." Burton jumped forward until I thought he might fall onto the ground, but he clung to his chair and he whispered the words at us, with those eyes of his burning into our frail hearts. "'Fire!'" he whispered. "'Fire on board!'

"I tell you, lads, it rattles the foundations of your mortal soul, and you feel the infinite calling to you with all the fears of all the ages wrapped into one tiny wooden trap all around you, the hell of time flaring and flinging toward her end, with no more repetitions or routines in sight, just a burning wooden bark, sinking down into a saltwater infinity. Time has come at you at last, lads, and you've got to choose, to burn quickly in a fast furious burst, or to drown slowly in your own frigid exhaustion. Fire or water. How will you go out, my boys, how will you choose to go out, when you hear that call rousing you from your sweet, gentle sleep in the night? 'Fire!' It will catch your breath away, lads. 'Fire on board!'"

Then Burton flopped back into his chair and he roared a deep, booming laughter. If he'd jumped up and said "Boo!" right then, I know I'd have fled that tent, with Robbie running right behind me. But he stopped laughing and listened for a moment to the night crickets. Then he said, "I can see it now, as if it was tonight. I looked down in the bunk below me, and even with the running and shouting on the decks above us, my Ciccio was still sound asleep. For a moment, I thought he was dead, lads. But then I saw that his mouth hung open and he was dragging in deep breaths without snoring. Great swallows of air were filling his lungs, and he was somewhere else, dreaming sweetly.

"So I jumped down onto the shifting floor and I shook him awake. 'Fire, Ciccio,' I said with my hands on his shoulders. 'Fire on the ship.' His dark eyes opened and without a pause or a thought he rolled out of his bunk and onto his bare feet, with the blanket still wrapped around his shoulders. His deep calm came from years and years of battle, all around the world. At the sound of alarm, he just awoke and arose and was ready to fight, even when he wasn't sure where he was or who his enemy might be.

"'Where is it?' he asked, standing beside me but coming only up to my shoulders. I had never noticed before how short he was. But mortal danger does that to you, ragazzi, you see things you've never noticed before, right before your eyes. 'I don't know,' I said. But he had already heard the calls of Aguiar over the scrambling feet pounding above us on the decks. He said nothing else, just climbed up the stairs and out onto the main deck, with that blanket still wrapped around his shoulders. As we came up from below, onto the tossing seas amidships, the winds caught his blanket and waved it in the air like a cape. He hung onto it with one hand and with the other he held himself steady by grasping a railing. His knees were bent a little, and his bare feet clung flat to the wooden deck, and he seemed to ride with the pitching brig like she was a galloping horse. I couldn't help but admire his sturdy sea legs, for I was clinging with both my hands to the rim of the stairs, almost down on my all fours, trying to stay aboard her in the storm.

"What we saw out on those decks of the Speranza, my boys, rolling out before us, awash with the retreating waves and buffeted by the winds, it was surely a vision of Hell itself, lads. Surely frigid, wind swept Hell itself.

"The decks were crowded with men, soaked to the bones, grasping at one another in panic, rushing to and fro, screaming like the gates of Old Dante's Hell had opened to swallow us all. Here there were three of them, nearly naked, clinging to some loose shred of the rigging. There a man, flat on his stomach, was washed across the deck until only a railing kept him aboard. Such screaming and open terror I'd never witnessed before. Not in all my years at sea.

"A group of six men clung to a stanchion by the hold, and out of the belly of the ship poured a huge cloud of black smoke, obscuring parts of the brig as she pitched back and forth. A white, frothy wave would crash onto the deck, grasping at the men. The cold water would pull that poor soldier on his stomach back from the railing and then sweep him across the deck again, his arms waving in the air, searching for anything he could hold onto, but reaching nothing. And then the sea would slosh down into the hold, only to be met by a rush of steam, mixed inextricably with the bellows of smoke crowding up out of the bowels of the ship and into the low, black skies."

Burton stopped there, lowered his eyes and looked again at something in his memory. After a moment, he said, "These were the men of the Italian Legion, boys. They'd survived the siege of Montevideo, the battle of the

Rio Grande de Sul and Costa Brava, they'd braved the great retreat of the Salto. They'd stared at death, and worse, at dismemberment and destruction, on battlefields across South America. Hardened veterans they were, lads. The men of the Italian Legion. But I can't describe to you what it means to be far, far out at sea, with your world ablaze on a wooden ship. The men of the Italian Legion, hardy and brave and true, ready to charge into the bayonets of the Oppressor, they were racked with pure terror, I tell you. There was no order, it was pandemonium, and yet, there was nowhere to flee, not for any of us. Staring out there from the top of the stairs, for me there was only a simple decision to be made: to drown or to burn. Perhaps, in even greater agony, to do both, if I didn't have the courage to decide.

"There came a moment then, just a pause, when the water retreated and the deck of the Speranza seemed nearly level. Out of that absurd moment of peace and calm, the sounds of all those men, and all their terror, bellowed up out of the ship like the smoke and steam rising out of her hold, cries from lost souls into the black and indifferent storm.

"That terrible noise was enough to freeze a man into place, my friends, but I saw my Zio suddenly rushing straight across the decks from the hold, and I rose up on my feet and followed him as closely as I could. Over the general rancor and disarray, I heard Aguiar's deep voice, and it dawned on me that Ciccio was headed toward his call, with me in tow, though he knew it not.

"As the brig suddenly pitched to the starboard, Ciccio disappeared down into the hold. I thought for a moment he'd fallen, or even been washed overboard. Yet with an instinct I barely understand, lads, an instinct we all label devotion, I followed him down into the smoke and steam in the belly of the ship. I chose the fire, because my Ciccio did.

"Below, in the hold, everything was surprisingly clear. Once I had pierced blindly through the clouds of smoke, I opened my eyes and found myself in the lowest part of the hold, with a strong course of wind blowing through my hair. I guess the fire had created some funnel of air to channel the smoke up through the lid of the hold, like a sort of smokestack. Down there, Aguiar and the General and three other men were fighting the flames with buckets and wet blankets.

" The fire was smaller than it seemed from above, from the volume of smoke it hurled upward, onto the deck of the brig. Still it burned hot and intensely, and it licked at the stores of our food, the dried meat and fruits and the hard tack stacked in bundles. Alongside the food, it blazed hottest at one point, and in the next instant it was clear to me what the problem was.

"In a corner of the hold there were cases of brandy stacked a couple of crates high. Not many, only six or so it seemed. But the two of them closest to the barrels of foodstuffs were at the center of the fire. Somehow, someone had set this brandy afire.

"My Zio ran in his bare feet over to the General, and some words I couldn't hear above the uproar were exchanged. Then Ciccio took a bucket from Aguiar's hands and doused himself with seawater.

"Oh, my lads, you never saw such a thing as what happened next. Ciccio threw that wet blanket over his head until it draped over his arms too, like he was playing at some gray ghost, he strode barefoot right up to the fire, blind beneath the wet blanket. He picked up the two offending crates of brandy and instantly ran straight up the plank and out of the hold of that brig. Aguiar ran just a step ahead of him, his booming voice calling out, 'Qui! Qui! Qui!' And by that he led Ciccio safely across the rocking deck of the ship.

"There was a moment when the eyes of the General met mine. But then without thinking I simply followed Ciccio's path. I picked up the next two crates of alcohol, and I followed behind Aguiar and my Zio, up the planking and out of the hold. I could see where I was running though, because the crates of brandy I carried were not on fire.

"Ciccio blindly collided into the rails and into the grasp of Aguiar, who held him aboard, and my Zio hurled the two blazing crates of liquor overboard and into the riled sea. It was no sooner overboard, than Aguiar had thrown him down onto the deck, and together they rolled to and fro, to put out the fire and free him from the smoldering blanket. In that same moment I hurled the two other crates of brandy in my arms overboard as well."

Jack Burton paused then and he set the lap desk down on the rug floor of the tent. Then he shook his head at something in his memory, and he laughed at it. "I'll not ever live that down," he whispered softly, speaking only to himself. Then he looked up at us and said, "No, that's not true. I guess, by God, I have. Haven't I? I have lived it down, boys. I have. Like everything else, I've outlived it."

We had not the slightest idea at that moment what he was rambling on about. But that didn't give Robbie a moment's pause. "Did you put the fire out?" Robbie said, out of his own held breath.

"Il Generale did, mi' ragazzo. He and those other three men with him. But not before we lost a lot of our food, and much of it spoiled in the equatorial heat over the next few weeks. It made for a longer voyage for us, ragazzi. We had, after that night, to ration out the stores carefully. And we got pretty hungry, we did, by the time we made the coast of Spain."

"But at least you didn't burn up and sink, sir," Robbie said.

Burton first grinned at him, and then for some reason at me, because I suppose my eyes were as big as my brother's about then. Jack Burton had a good laugh then, though the fondness in his eyes didn't disappear.

"It's true. But it was hard on my Zio Ciccio, boys. I tried to save the best of my share for him, but even that was too little, and going rotten, and not good. It made it worse for him."

"Did he get burnt up?" Robbie said.

"No. It was just really that.   See, after I'd pitched my crates of fine, sealed brandy overboard, I hit the deck too, helping Aguiar. At first I thought Zio was burned, boys, because he seemed to be thrashing around in Aguiar's grasp. But as I held him too, and beat the flames around him away I thought, while waves of saltwater washed over us, soaking us down in every thread we wore, I realized that my Ciccio wasn't writhing in pain from the flames, or struggling to put out the heat, he was wracked with coughing. He was coughing himself to death, lads."

Burton reached down beside his wheelchair and picked up that bottle of wine he had set there, but he didn't drink from it right away. He just held it for a while, and he looked over at Zambutto Sammy. "E' stanco, Sammy" he cooed at the animal, and he reached out a hand a stroked the ape's great brow again. The gorilla lowered his head a bit, basking in the man's touch.

"What was wrong with him?" I asked.

"My Ciccio?" Burton asked, glancing over at me. "Mio caro Ciccio," he sang out in a whispered breath.

"Yes," I said.

"It wasn't the fire, lad. Though the fire didn't do him any good. No. And it wasn't the rotting food we had for weeks then aboard our Speranza, and the little of it to go around. But that didn't do him any good either. No." Finally Burton took a long swallow from the wine, and when he finally went on, he gazed down at the bottle in his hands as if it was a last, desperate distraction.

"We all gave him the best part of our rations, you know. And nobody more than the General. There were days, I think, when the General ate little more than a handful trimmed off the edges of the rot, because he gave everything that was any good to Francesco.

"I know I was hungry, but I gave him the best of what we had. Still his eyes just grew darker and more shaded by his brow, and the little cough was persistent. Always there, lurking just behind every word he said. He kept on with my reading lessons, but at times he'd have to stop and cough and cough and cough, until we had to quit.

" In the evenings, under the stars on the deck, Il Generale would lead us in the singing, and we all got a draught of the brandy that was left. He did this, the General, to keep the fires of freedom burning in our hearts, because now the voyage was months on, and growing long. And we were hungry.

"And dear Ciccio, he would insist on standing amidships and singing right along. But even though he had part of my draught of brandy, and usually all of the General's too, and even Aguiar's, too, sometimes he would start to cough and it wouldn't stop, and we would end up carrying him down to his bunk below, Aguiar and I. His arms around our shoulders, but his whole body thrown and tossed by the coughing, until he curled up in a ball in the bed, trying to hold himself still, but shaking with the hard rhythm of his cough"

"What was it?" Robbie said.

Burton ignored us then. He was somewhere else and the disease of his soul didn't need a name for the disease of his friend. He said, "One night, mi' ragazzi, after Ciccio had fallen asleep, I was standing alone at the stern of the brig, watching the wake diminish and disappear behind us out on the Atlantic, when Aguiar wandered up after his watch, and stood there beside me. He had a cigar in his mouth, and he chewed on the end of it, but he didn't light it. It was one of the General's, and there were only a few left, so Aguiar wouldn't waste it by lighting it except every once in a while. Mostly he just held it in his lips and chewed on it.

"But he stood there beside me, with one long arm cast up in the rigging, holding that cigar to his lips, moving it around with his other hand and tasting the tobacco, and I asked him just that, because I was confused. 'What is it?' I said. I don't know that I believed he could answer me. It was really just a plea.

"But he told me then about my friend Anzani, and how he had traveled the world, lads, fighting wherever he could in behalf of Liberty. Wherever in the world some small band was standing up against the lords for their freedom and their equality, no matter how slim their odds were, that was where my Zio stood. Francesco Anzani." Burton nodded his head with a confident air at that.

"'He's not been home to Italy in over twenty seven years' Aguiar said. That tall man, as black as the moonless sky, eyed me then, measuring me as if I was a boy. But there was no way he could know my history, understand how old I was. It was impossible. Because it is impossible.

"'Ciccio was a student,' Aguiar said to me. 'He was studying the course in mathematics at the University in Pavia, and he was a smart young man, il piccolo. He'd have gone far if he'd stayed, he'd have become a professor or a scientist. But Anzani has a heart that is too big for that, il piccolo.' That's what Aguiar called me, il piccolo, if he had only known.

"But that was the year when the Greeks rose up to fight for their independence. And my Ciccio, he left the university and the easy, learned life and he went to fight for their liberty. For the independence of Greece. This is what Aguiar told me about my Ciccio, while we stood in the stern of the Speranza."

Robbie floated up onto his knees and clapped his hands together. And I couldn't help it, because I was sitting straight up too. At that moment, filled with the drama the lurked in Burton's eyes and spurred on his speech, filled with our own little excitement, we startled the ape out of his drugged lethargy over on his little stool. He lifted his head and snorted once or twice in confusion.

Burton just laughed at the two of us, and I guess at old Zambutti Sam too. He reached out and patted the ape's broad brow again, and then laughed a bit more at my brother and me.

"Woe, miei ragazzi, woe! Don't get too excited! Let me tell you the whole of his story, before you get too ready to run off from your school days. See, Aguiar says to me that night, 'He could never go home to Italia. After he fought with the Greeks, he was an exile. He was a man with no home, a man with no country.' You boys, you are too young to know what that means, to wander through time across the face of this dark earth with no place to call a home. Hunted by the names and the families and the things you've done in your past, with nowhere but inside your own shoes to live, it is a terrifying thing, O ragazzi, no matter how old you grow. How can I tell you poor lads how this is?" Burton said more to himself than to us, mournfully. "You boys can never know this. You have a home in this world, you do."

I was still up on my knees, but Robbie in front of me seemed to sink down a little as Burton spoke. And suddenly I felt the weariness of the night pressing on me.

"My Ciccio, he spoke to me once of this, boys, 'Whenever peace comes, that place is no longer my home. I will always search in every other part of this world for the battles that will devour me.' This is what he told me, boys. For the battles that will devour us. It was his passion, and it was his curse."

At that Burton fell silent and, gazing blankly at the tent walls around us, his hand touched the big animal beside him. Zambutti Sam snorted again and moved over from his low stool onto the rug that lay on the ground beside Burton. Then like a loyal old dog, the ape leaned quietly against the strange man in his wheelchair.

As I watched, I sank down onto the floor too. I was too young then to know the destitution and the loneliness he must have felt, or even to recognize what it was. But I felt it, even if I didn't understand it, and Robbie did too. After the fires of leaving school to fight for liberty, this heavy cost, whatever it was, it weighed down hard upon us, weighed us to the ground.

"He went from Greece on to Spain, Aguiar told me, and then from there he fought for the liberali in Portugal. From one struggle on to the next, he went, without a home. With no home but the battlefield in all the world's guerilla wars. That's what we call them now, lads, guerilla wars. Back then, it was just the only way to resist. 'It was there, in Iberia, that he was wounded the first time,' Aguiar said to me, and as he spoke on the deck of the Speranza, he pointed with the long finger of his hand to his own side, under his left arm. 'He keeps the wound hidden, you know, and he won't show it to you. He'll even deny it if you ask him, but somewhere there in Spain or Portugal, a bayonet got him, and it had to be deep in the lung. And that, il piccolo, that was the start of all this.'

"What Aguiar meant was the coughing and the weakness and that dark shadow that drifted over his eyes at night sometimes, most times by then. You see, the wounds from his fighting in Iberia had led to the consumption that was slowly eating up his lungs.

"Aguiar told me, in the days when they'd first fought in Uruguay, for the Republic of Rio Grande, that my Ciccio could hide his illness. 'He was young, and strong as a wild pony, and he could run and ride and fight with the best of us. The General never knew, not for the longest time, not for years,' Aguiar told me. 'But slowly it caught up with Francesco, and we began to see him change. He was turning in earlier at night, drinking too much wine to deaden the pain, and then, finally, running out of breath. I was there, il piccolo, the night il Generale cornered him and asked him what was wrong. That was when he showed the General his old wound. It is still the only time I've seen it,' said Aguiar. 'And so now, my friend,' Aguiar, who would die defending Rome, said to me, 'now we have come to this.'"

Burton grew quiet again, and seemed to go somewhere that my little brother and I couldn't follow. Then suddenly, he breathed in deep once and said to the ape, "Butto, mia pipa." The gorilla moved aside and then lifted and handed over the little chest to Burton. The red shirt lay folded carefully on top of it, and when Burton put a hand on it he paused. "I haven't spoken about my dear Ciccio in a long, long while," he said, as if he was talking to himself, as if he was trying to explain away something that he dared not try to understand, not even from a great distance.

Then he began the ritual with the pipe again, in silence this time, until he had warmed the bowl and lit it and swallowed hard and whole the sweet white smoke, and again passed it over to the ape who smoked the last of it and then carefully scraped the bowl clean, eating every crumb of the resins.

"I don't do this every night," Burton muttered, staring down into his lap, "almost never twice." He sat back in the wheeled chair and closed his eyes. His chin was lifted a bit in the air, and he appeared to sleep for a while, though once in that time he muttered the name "Anzani." Zambutti Sam tucked away the cleaned pipe and all of its accoutrements in the little chest, and smoothed the folded red shirt over its top. And through it all, even in the dreamy quiet, Robbie and I were riveted to the scene before us. The whole tent seemed to us to be part of some wild other world, and our little house in our small hometown and all the Mrs. Coogan's of the world seemed to drop away like so much sweat in a darkened steam bath. I think now, as I look back on that night, it may have been the traces of that sweet white sunset smoke that lingered in the air like incense at a holy mass, it may have been that which took us all so far away. The journey, the real one we still wander on, had begun. Yet it may just have been the traces of that crazy smoke.

I don't know how long we were like that. Time had become an illusion to me then. But after a while had passed, Burton began to speak to us again, as if we were emerging from an old dream and his story had become our common reality. The tent lay in total darkness, with only the soft glow of the heater lighting our faces and the glimmering of our eyes.

"One night, as my reading lesson was ending, and dear Ciccio seemed so tired, he began to cough. And his coughing went on. And it wouldn't stop. Eventually he curled over on his side in his bunk, and blood began to leak from the corner of his mouth, and hard black clots of it came up from his lungs. I was wiping up the stained sheets with a rag, my hand resting on Ciccio's trembling shoulder. Aguiar got up and ran off to the mess, and he came back with the General behind him and the last of the brandy. The General took my place beside Anzani at his bunk, and fed him the brandy slowly until he settled down and the coughing stopped. The General wiped at the sweat on Ciccio's brow, and that care alone seemed to quiet him, though I know it was the brandy slowly sinking in, letting him rest.

"'That's the end of it,' Aguiar said plaintively. 'The last of the brandy we've got left on board.'

"'We're only a day or two out of Spagna,' the General said, as he was ever the optimist. Then my Ciccio laughed out loud.

"'What is it, Francesco?' the General said, smiling down at Caro Ciccio and gently mopping the sweat from his brow. There was a deep, old fondness between those two men, for they had so long been brothers, comrades in the same long struggle.

"Ciccio chuckled a little, and then he said, 'You mean to tell me, mi' Generale, that we would have had all the brandy we could drink, all the way across the wide, wide Atlantic, if only my little Burtoni here wouldn't have thrown the half of it away?'

"The General and Aguiar laughed together, and I confessed, 'But Ciccio,' I pleaded, 'I was only following your lead!'

"'Ah, il piccolo,' said my Zio. 'But what I threw away was on fire!' He coughed a few times, but ever so gently now, and a bit controlled. 'You tossed the good stuff overboard!'

"Aguiar clapped me on the shoulder from behind, and I heard his big laugh rumble out, and then the General's too. 'If I hadn't needed to catch you, Francesco, and keep you from going right on overboard, I might have tackled the little one and saved at least a bottle, maybe even two,' Aguiar said.

"It was good for all of us, for Zio Ciccio especially, to laugh. And not to think about his deep, hoarse cough and his blood staining the sheets.

"'Soon,' said the General, 'soon, we'll all be sipping sweet Spanish wine, and soaking up the sun on the shores of our dear, old Mediterranean Sea.'

"And as the General said it would be, so it was."

A broad smile spread across Burton's lips, and he gazed up over our heads at some Mediterranean place in his long memory. "That was a day, O ragazzi. Oh, that was a day. We sailed on an easy wind right through the straits of Gibraltar and we put in, on a shining, sunny afternoon to the port of Santa Pola, on the south coast of Spain.

"He orderd us not to go ashore, to stay on board, for we needed to press on toward Italia. But the men argued with him, after months at sea. 'Let us go put our feet on the ground,' we cried out. Still he held to a higher plan, our Generale. He sent Gazzolo, the ship's captain, ashore alone to see about supplies, and then he went below to see how Ciccio was doing. 'Do you need to go ashore?' the General asked only Francesco. 'Do you need a rest?'

"'Mi' Generale, are we not headed for Italia?' was Ciccio's reply, and I thought an argument between these two old friends might rightly ensue. But right then we all heard the shouts of the men above us, 'Liberta'! Liberta'!' they cried. And over that came the voice of Captain Gazzolo, 'Generale! Generale!' he cried.

"As the General rose from my Ciccio's bedside, Gazzolo came barreling down the stairs, with Aguiar right behind him, both of them breathing hard, and the both of them came up short at the sight of the General, and they stood at attention.

"'What is it?' he said.

"O! Miei ragazzi, what a day that was," Burton said, and he laughed and laughed. He shook his head to and fro and his eyes winced shut in pure joy.

"What was it?" Robbie said, after we grew tired of listening to Burton's laughter.

"What was it?" I said.

Burton stopped and he looked over at us, and his hand reached over and touched the red cloth resting on little chest filled with his smoking implements. His smile now wrinkled into a twist of amusement. "Ah, my boys, may you have many days in your lives like that fine day in mine. Days you remember with great joy for all of your time.

"You see, the Captain held in his hands a dozen or so pages of some Spanish newspaper, pages that someone had carefully clipped out and saved. Some patriot stranded on the shores of far off Spain, like the General and my Ciccio had been stranded in Montevideo, some exile, hiding in Spain from the aristocrats and the church, waiting for il Generale's return. Someone had saved this pressing news, hoping against hope itself for our return.

"'Oh, mi' Generale, it has started! Look!' Captain Gazzolo cried. 'Read, mi' Generale, read!' And he shoved the sheaf of papers in his hands at him.

"Ciccio lifted himself up on one arm from his bunk, and suddenly his darkened eyes seemed brighter. 'It has started, Francesco,' Gazzolo said to him.

"'The revolution,' Aguiar said from behind the Captain, 'It's the revolution, Anzani.'

"Gazzolo nodded his head in agreement. 'We have come home at just the right moment,' he said. Meanwhile the General was reading through the papers with a furious glare, shuffling them like he was holding a hand of cards dealt from history's deck, lads. He was eager to see what was on the page that followed, then shuffling back to be sure he had read the news on the first page right.

95

"'What is it?' said my Zio to him, as he sat up in his bunk. Above us I heard the furious pounding of feet on the decks, and the chants of 'Liberta'!' The men were dancing with some old, wild frenzy on the decks amidships.

"The General lifted his eyes from the newspaper and gazed over at his old comrade-in-arms, Francesco Anzani. He wore no smile, and his eyes were fierce. 'We have risen in Milano, Francesco. We have taken the city back from the Austrians.' And he handed the papers over to my Ciccio, with the pounding feet on the decks above him like the rattling of drums, and the voices of the men faint above that, singing old hymns in Italian.

"'And in Napoli, and in Venice,' said Aguiar, grinning, his arms akimbo.

"Captain Gazzolo stamped a foot on the wooden floor, and said to the General, 'Emperor Louis-Phillippe is gone from Paris, and the Metternich is gone from Vienna. And the Croat soldiers of Austria have fled from the streets of Milano.' Then he raised a tight fist in the air before him.

"Ciccio just stared down at the newspapers and his feet touched the floor beneath his bunk. He looked over at me, as I tried to follow what all this talk meant, and my Zio said, "It has begun, il piccolo. The renaissance of our people has started at last.' Then he paused before he and the General said, quietly and instinctively, and almost at the same moment, 'Viva Italia!'

"That was the moment, O ragazzi. In all of our joy, that was the moment when their great misunderstanding began. It would mark Il Generale for the rest of his many long days, still it was nothing but a mistake. And yet, I will never forget that wonderful moment, filled with such verve and spirit, yet eternally darkened by a simple mistake between these two old friends."

Burton stopped there, he looked down and seemed to see the ground under us, beneath the carpet, the simple dirt.

Then he spoke to himself, I think. We could barely hear him, it was so soft. "Neither of those two great men knew how much they loved one another." He shook his head back and forth, just tiny millimeters, and just for a brief instant. "They never knew," he whispered. "They died without really knowing what it all meant."

"What happened?" I asked, and both Burton and the ape behind him looked up at me, as if they were surprised to see me sitting there, so deep were they both in the fog of their smoke, and for Burton so deep in his memories. Robbie glanced back at me, he was up on his knees now, and he looked worried.

"What happened, sir?" he repeated.

Burton rested back in his wheelchair and seemed tired and old for the first time that night. You could see the doubts in his eyes, did he want to go on, to tell us the hard part, the part about the failures and the death. What happened when the glorious voyage was over, with all its hopes and dreams, until only defeat and despair lurked ahead of them.

"My Ciccio," was all he said, and his eyes closed on the world.

I guess we let him sit there in his wheelchair, looking older than the giant elms scattered around the schoolyard, trees that were soon to grow streaked with death and ill and then to be cut down and burned in order to desperately and vainly try to defeat the disease that was spreading through the land. We left him alone for a time, and Zambutti Sam stirred in his little stool, and gazed on Burton with warm, steadfast eyes that told even me, with my few years, that this was not the first night Jack Burton had taken to his pipe in order to ease himself off into his sleep.

"Sir?" Robbie said to him softly, and Burton's eyes opened slowly. He looked at us, uncomprehending for a moment. But I knew then he wasn't sleeping, or absent. He was just deep and deeper in his memories.

"Carlo Alberto," he said.

"Who was that?" I said, and Robbie sat back on his heels, and then as Burton began again to tell us the story, Robbie tilted back over to this side and rested his weight on an arm.

I realized that I was lying back now with my head cradled in my hands, my legs stretched out in front of me toward the glowing propane heater. Singing behind old Burton's yarn was the music of crickets and the now and then snort or the shake of a mane from the circus horses staked outside in the playground.

"That night, resting off the coast of Spain," Burton went on, "in the safe harbor of Santa Pola, the men were dancing on the decks of the Speranza. And my Ciccio, he was sitting up in the bed, his feet were again touching the boards of the floor, his coughing had died down and the blood at the corners of his mouth had been wiped away, gone from his lips. And then the General said to him, 'Carlo Alberto has declared war on the Austrians, Francesco, and his army has marched into Lombardy, to come to the aid of the Milanese.'

"'Viva Italia!' shouted Captain Gazzolo."

"Who was he?' said Robbie, because like me, he was suddenly lost. And we had never seen an adult behave this way, not in all our lives. Adults were supposed to be clear headed and certain and in charge, telling us what to do, whether we liked it or not. Adults were not supposed to be filled with dreams and yearning for lost lands and distant wars. That was for kids and people in the movies, not for adults.

Burton stared blankly past us, speaking as if to ghosts, as he explained, "Carlo Alberto was the King of Sardinia, my boys, with an army of 60,000 men. And he led these men into Lombardia, and declared war on the Austrian oppressors. He came to help the rebels who were rising in Milano and Venezia. So the war for Italy had begun for real, ragazzi, and Carlo Alberto meant to unify it all under the House of Savoy. It would all become the Kingdom of Sardinia, and the Frenchmen and the Austrian hussars would all be gone. That is who Carlo Alberto was: King Carlo Alberto of Sardinia.

"So, you see, lads, Aguiar and the Captain gave out a great shout then. 'Viva Italia!' they cried, and this brought a big grin to the General's lips, an old warrior's grin, filled with hail fellow-feeling and grand victory dreams.

"Il Generale stood straighter then it seemed to me, and he said to Gazzolo, 'No time to go ashore, Captain. Do we have the supplies to make for Nizza?'

"'We will, my General. There is a boat on its way at this moment, bearing us the water and food we need. Given to us by the patriots of Santa Pola.'

"I saw the General glance over at my Ciccio, and he seemed surprised. You see, my boys, my Zio's head had once again sunk down into his shoulders a little, though he stared hard at the General. And this again made the General, and the rest of us, worry.

"'We must sail straight on for Nizza, Captain,' the General said. 'We need to make shore and join with the armies of the King.' But the General kept his eyes cautiously on my Ciccio as he spoke, and never looked over at Captain Gazzolo. 'Is there brandy for my friend Francesco on that boat that is coming so soon, Captain?' he asked, his gaze never leaving my Ciccio for a moment.

"'Yes, sir,' said the Captain.

"'Good,' the General replied, and then finally he squared his shoulders and turned toward my dear Zio and asked him, 'Are you sure you are well enough to go on, Francesco? Do you need now to go ashore here?'

"My Zio shook his head no, violently shook it, lads. 'To Italia,' he said, but still he kept staring at the General, and his head hung weakly from his shoulders.

"'What is it, my friend?' the General said, seeing my Ciccio's agitation. 'What's wrong, Francesco? Is it something the brandy won't kill?'

"'Yes, Peppino,' Ciccio said, and he looked away from the General. 'It is something that your brandy can't kill.'

"'Then,' the General said, 'what is it?'

"'It is this King,' he said, 'this Carlo Alberto.'

"I looked over toward Aguiar and at the Captain, because you see, lads, I didn't understand. But this was a new tone in my Zio's voice. There was a heavy moment of silence, and then it was broken by the General's laughter. And that broad laughter of his sealed the freight of their misunderstanding. It would lie in the hold of both their ears as long as they lived, though it was just the laughter of a moment, it was like a weighted cargo filled with the lead of disappointment."

Burton stopped there, and with his face cast downward onto the dim light, his eyes gazed up from beneath his gray brow, and stared hard and still at something just above our heads and in the distant past. But nothing was there.

"Ciccio was fierce as he spoke out then, and his voice cut through the General's laughter, and silenced it at once. 'There are no more Kings,' Francesco Anzani spat out. He sounded as he spoke as if he would never need to cough again.

"The General paused for a moment, and then he tried to explain to his friend, 'Francesco, first we will make a country, first we must create Italia. Then, when we have won our unity and Italia is clear and on every map in all the world, then we will see about our King. Don't you see, Francesco? We will use Carlo Alberto and his armies and his treasure and his Kingdom of Sardinia to make ourselves into a country, a real country, that reaches from Sicilia to Nizza, a country of our own.'

"As the General spoke, his head reared high and his voice rose, the way only his voice could, and it stirred around in my soul, and I knew then, lads, I knew I would follow him anywhere he needed me to go, and I could see in the light behind the eyes of Aguiar and Captain Gazzolo that it was true for them too. He would lead us on toward victory, and to the glory we could only dream of, and we knew it was so. Our hearts sang and told us it was so.

"But it was not so for my Ciccio.

"Short, little Ciccio Anzani got up on his feet and stood chest to chest with the General, though he seemed tiny and helpless when he did it. But the anger in his face made all the veins in his neck tight. 'Peppino,' he said, 'My friend Peppino.' And that word 'friend' was buried under the irony of his hard tone. 'There are no kings, Peppino.' His head nodded to emphasize his every word. 'You are dancing with a demon, my General. And this demon, he will take away . . . '

"But that was as far as my Ciccio could go. I had never seen him so angry before, and the fire in his heart broke then, lads, and he collapsed back down onto his bunk, and suddenly he began to cough and cough and the spasms of mucus in his chest rattled and shook, and he leaned over sideways and again the blood began to leak from his lips. I took hold of his shoulder and tried to hold him still, but he rocked and shook with the slow rupture in his lungs.

"But the General did not move to his bedside. He glared down at him, with a fury unbroken in his eyes, and he did something then, I know it, boys, I know he would regret it for the rest of his days. He turned, with a rolling horseman's turn on his heel, and he strode right past Aguiar and Gazzolo and climbed back up to the deck, where his men were dancing for joy and for freedom.

"And when he reached the top of the stair, he stopped looked back down at us, at Aguiar and at me holding my Ciccio's trembling shoulders. 'Captain,' he snapped, not addressing us but Gazzolo. 'Those supplies.' he said. 'On board yet?'

"Then he turned on his heel again and disappeared above us. Aguiar helped me as we eased my Zio back down into his bunk, and the Captain, with a clipped nod to Aguiar, followed the General onto the deck.

"My Zio was so weak then, and too angry to do much of anything but lie there and try to find stillness, try to ease his lungs into not a peace but a quiet. Aguiar must have seen the confusion and the fear in my eyes, because he laid one hand on my shoulder. And I felt the warmth of it like a comfort.

"'King,' my Ciccio spat out with his blood on the dank sheets.

"'Rest,' said Aguiar, his hand still on my shoulder, and speaking not just to the sick man, but to us all. 'Rest now.'"

Burton didn't really pause so much as he shifted back in his chair then. He scruffed at the short gray hair on his head, and a smile returned to his face. "In just a few days the Speranza arrived in Nice. Now, back then, ragazzi, a ship coming in from a voyage across the sea, it should have been quarantined for days, but not the Speranza. As we sailed into the harbor in Nice, we were met by hundreds at the fort proclaiming 'Long Live il Generale! 'Long Live il Generale!' Oh, they sang out all around us.

"And on the first boat plowing toward us, among the dozen headed to the ship, stood the General's wife. She was tall and slim, and her hair was thick and deep nut brown almost black, and so thick it had a life of its own. Where he was all blonde and burnt rose by the weather, Anita was olive and brown, with just a hint of the Amazon in the cast of her dark eyes.

"And, oh, my boys, there would be no quarantining of the Speranza. Not with bold Anita leading the hundreds on the shore into the little boats to greet us, surrounded by the cheers of the volunteers on the land and on board the ship. It seemed in no time, surrounded by the whirl of the volunteers, that we were carried ashore."

"What about Ciccio?" Robbie said. "Was he cheering too? Was he carried too?"

"Yes, my boy," Burton smiled at him with a paternal glow, "Anita had my Ciccio carried off to the house where she was staying, the house of the General's mother. And so the mother and the wife took to caring for him. I slept in the summer warmth out in a little piazza, before their house, but I spent my time there beside my Ciccio. His eyes, over those days, grew clearer and he sat up and drank soups and ate bread that the General's mother made for him. And there was red, red wine, filled with breath and life, to be had. And, maybe it was just that this soldier, this cavalryman from all the world's armies, maybe he grew better because his feet were back on solid ground, and he could dream again of being astride a horse. Whatever it was, we all began to feel better, watching my Ciccio recover."

"Where was the General?" I said.

"Did they make friends again?" said Robbie.

"Oh, there was no time to wait, not for the General, much as he would have loved to sit up of an evening, with his children around him, with his dearest Anita, in his mother's house where he'd spent his own baby days, and drink that dark red wine 'till late in the night with his friends Francesco and Aguiar. But for him there was a country to be won, a revolution to stir to life, and liberty to be had for his land, like the liberty in America and in France.

"No, he and his legion of men, which over those first few nights I believed included me and my Zio, they were headed for Genova. In just a few days, the Speranza was readied and the men were waiting to charge forward, as they listened every night around the hearth fires of Nice to the news and the stories coming back from Milano and Venezia of revolution and rebellion. In two or three days, the General was set to return to Genova, to the heartland, to find King Carlo Alberto and offer him the services of this General and his Italian Legion, veterans all from the wars of South America.

"In the evening of the next day, he found me outside, sitting in the shade of his mother's house, tossing marbles in the dust of the piazza with some of his children. 'Burtoni,' he said to me, and led me aside, away from the children and from that child's play. It was the first time he'd spoken directly to me, and used my name, too. 'Burtoni,' he said. So I knew it meant he had orders for me."

Jack Burton grinned again at that memory, and then he told us, "Il Generale was more clever than I realized then." And Burton laughed to himself. "He said to me, 'Francesco seems to be feeling better, no?'

"'I think so, sir,' I answered him.

"'I have seen the way he watches after you, Burtoni,' the General nodded his head and gazed straight into my eyes. 'And the way you look out for him.'

"I muttered 'Yes, sir,' though it wasn't all that clear to me.

"'But, I have to tell you, though this is hard, he's not well enough to come with us, Burtoni,' Il Generale frowned. 'It would be the end of him, I'm afraid, if he tried to come' He stopped, and then he looked even deeper into my eyes and I knew again that I would follow him into whatever battle he led me, however lost or hopeless, wherever he led me, I would go. But then, lads, he said the impossible thing.

"'I need you to stay here with him, Burtoni. It would be good for you to come with the Legion, to join us in the revolution, but what I need is for you to stay here with our dear Anzani. It will be the only way that I can convince him to stay in Nice, with my mother and Anita. So that he can get well.'

"'But!' I said.

"But it was an order. And I knew it.

"So the General clapped me hard on the shoulder, and then he promised me, 'We will meet again, Burtoni, in a new land. In a new country. Reborn from its ancient ruins. We will be together. And our dear friend Francesco Anzani, he will be standing beside us.'

"And so they all left, long before the earliest light, the Speranza carrying the Italian Legion of Montevideo off to the peninsula, in search of the revolution. And I was the one who woke my Zio in the morning with the news."

"Was he mad?" said Robbie.

Burton seemed more sad than amused, but a crooked, little whisper of a smile graced his lips. "Mad is not the word, ragazzi. He was not angry. That was not my Ciccio's way. He was not even disappointed, or even surprised. It was almost as if he expected as much from Il

Generale, and from me. So no, he wasn't angry. But he stood up out of his bed, and he dressed himself and he was filled with determination. He took some bread and a little milk mixed with coffee, and then he headed down the hill toward the port.

"I followed behind him, telling him repeatedly that we were under orders from the General to wait with his wife and mother, until the time was ripe for us all to return to Italia. We've been ordered to look after Anita and the family,' I pleaded with Ciccio as we stepped together out into the piazza.

"Clouds had rolled in over the morning sky, growing ever blacker in the west. 'Where are you going?' I said to him, just as big round drops of rain began to splat on the yellow stones around us.

"Ciccio laughed loud and turned to me, 'You've been ordered to look after me, Il Piccolo,' he said. "That's what you've been ordered. And I've been ordered—indirectly ordered, I must add—but ordered, still, to stay behind.' Then he rounded on his heel and strode down across the piazza toward the waterfront. His black hair, streaked now with gray, it blew back from his brow as he headed into the summer wind blowing up out of the morning sea.

"'Where are you going, Zio?' I said.

"'To see when the next ship can take me to Genova,' he shouted over his shoulder, with nary the sound of a cough. 'You stay here and take care of Mama.' I ran after him and as I caught up, he said, with his shoulders squared, 'Peppino doesn't think I can keep up with him. He's got a start on me, but he's forgotten what a heart I have.'

"As we made our way down to the docks, the wind rose and the rain broke hard and the storm that had been bearing toward us across the mountains of Spain came blowing full on. But the hard weather didn't even give Anzani a pause. My Zio strode right on, and we got ourselves drenched in the process, but we wound up standing, so wet Ciccio's hair dripped down his back and the drops just rolled off him because his red shirt was already completely soaked, and there was nothing for the water to do but roll off him, but yet we stood in the rain and he bought us tickets on a mail boat. He bought his passage to Genova. And when he was done, he looked at me and laughed and then handed me the coins to buy my own passage too.

"And that was how well we followed the General's orders."

Burton rubbed at his chin, and shook his head at something in his memory, then he went on, "As luck would have it, that same summer storm that drenched us drove the Speranza south, carrying the General and his Legion with it. But Ciccio and I hopped that old mail sloop in the afternoon and we made straight from Genova. We landed ahead of the Speranza, and so we met the crowds waiting at the docks. You see, lads, the word had run out ahead of us. The Italian Legion was coming, with the General at its head. And just as it was in Nice, a crowd was waiting for him in Genova.

"We came ashore, still damp and cold from the morning's rain. And me, looking like a kid, I tried to tell them all that we were with the Legion. That this was Francesco Anzani beside me, who had ridden and fought beside the General in Rio del Sol and defended the walls of Montevideo as a soldier in the General's Legion.

"But the Genovese, what they saw was a sick, weakened man, old before his years, and a cheeky young loudmouth. I tried to tell them different, but Anzani only smiled and kept his mouth shut, and he held his head high.

"'So why are you coming on this old mail tub, little soldier,' the Genovese laughed at my barking pride.

"My Ciccio only grinned at me and shook his head at my spouting off. He didn't say a word. He didn't need to say a word, because he had nothing to prove."

Burton laughed at himself, and then said, "I wasn't as young as I acted, or as young as I looked, ragazzi. But here is a lesson for you boys: Want to look like a youngster? Want to be treated like a green kid? Shoot your mouth off a lot, with no way to back up your word.

"I learned after that to keep still, like Francesco Anzani did, because what you do speaks for the ages, not what you say you did. And with what has happened to me," he stopped to laugh again. "With all that I've seen and done, nobody would believe me anyway. Not if I dared to tell all that I've seen and all that I've done."

He leaned slowly forward in his wheelchair, and his chest and shoulders seemed to press out of his shirt toward Robbie and me, and he said, "Do you, little ragazzi? Do you believe me?"

I saw Robbie's head nodding yes in front of me, and then Burton's gray eyes slipped over and held mine, and I said, "Yes," and I nodded like my little brother.

"I do, sir," said Robbie.

Burton laughed an evil laugh that made me wonder why I did believe him. But I can tell you, after all these years, I'm still hunting for traces of Jack Burton, wherever I go in the world. And I've never yet found any trace of Il Rosso that wasn't as hard to believe as this was, or even harder, and that wasn't also as true as life itself, as far as I could see.

*   *   *

Jack Burton reached back and took up the wine bottle and swallowed another draught. Then he set the bottle down, and he grew serious again.

"Night fell on the port of Genova then, and the salty breeze blowing in was cool, even in July, but Ciccio and I were still waiting with the restless crowd for the arrival of the Speranza. We'd eaten a little and shared a bottle of red wine, and our clothes were now mostly dry. Ciccio seemed tired, after the long day, but I guess the wine buoyed him up, because he never complained, and only rarely did he sit or rest. Mostly he wandered about the dock, always gazing at the horizon.

"There were lanterns lit on the waterfront, and it was a night like this one, summertime but cool and damp by the seaside. And then the first shout went up, 'Thar she be!' they sung out. 'The Speranza!' And men were suddenly straining to see around one another.

"I suppose it took an hour for the brig to come into port, and during that time the crowd around us grew and grew, and now and again a shout would roll up out of the men, 'Viva Italia!' or "Viva Milano!' And there developed a low and constant murmuring of men's voices, filled with anticipation and wonder. Around the edges of the crowd, the carabinieri had gathered, looking nervous but knowing all the time that this was a crowd beyond their control. Children, up past their bed times, they hid around the edges of the noisy crowd, hoping their mothers wouldn't notice." Burton stopped, grinned at the two of us, but said nothing.

"So it was, the Speranza sailed into port and she was tied down speedily, amidst the shouts and the cheers of the men, men on the docks and men on the streets of Genova, and men on the decks of the brig. One shout would bring on another, and then the answering call of another. But Ciccio and I, we stood quietly and watched our old ship settle into her moorings.

"After a while, with the men on board scurrying about, and the rounds of cheers rolling through the crowd and across the decks, the General strode up and stood in the prow of the Speranza, where he could look down on the assembled men, his countrymen, he would make them his countrymen, he would, and he stood where they all could see him, as well.

"The crowd knew him in a moment, because they recognized the red blouse and the long blond locks falling onto his shoulders, already the stuff of legend, it was. 'Viva!' the men on the docks yelled, 'Viva!'" Jack Burton yelled out those words in the schoolyard night, but we were so enchanted within his world, we did not jump or stir. We just listened, as we'd never listened before.

"The General stood there, his head high, with dark Aguiar dressed in the red blouse too and right at this shoulder, and then Il Generale raised his arms above his head with his palms out toward us, and at just that simple gesture the crowd fell completely silent.

"He spoke then, and he went on for a quarter of an hour or more, and whenever he paused to breathe, the shouts of the crowd rose up. But I didn't hear much of it, or I heard it, but I don't now remember much of what he said. I remember the shouts of the men on the decks behind him, and the men on the docks around Ciccio and me. But mostly I remember this.

"'Viva Italia!' the General said to start, and it caused an uproar. The Carabinieri behind us shuffled from foot to foot nervously, their hands touching their sidearms gently, checking they were ready, but some of them I think even joined in the cheers. My Zio held a fist in the air. I don't think he had the strength in his lung to shout, so that gesture was his cry. But his heart still felt strong, too strong. And then it happened.

"Il Generale, in the next moment he cried out in a shout over the noise of the crowd. 'Long Live Carlo Alberto,' he called to us, with fire in his eyes that I could see across the rows and rows of men's waving arms ahead of me. 'Viva Carlo Alberto,' he cried, and some men began to toss their caps in the air. Then the General held his left hand out, open and welcoming, as if to bring an old friend in close to his side. But there was no friend. And he would learn there would be no friend. There was only this operatic, flowing gesture, filling an emptiness beside him he couldn't see, lads, and yet there was his shout, 'Viva Carlo Alberto!'

"I saw my Ciccio grow rigid, and the fist he had in the air dropped to his side. The veins in his neck tightened again and, in a moment, his face turned feverishly red. And then, as the men shouted 'Viva Re!' all around us, Ciccio collapsed onto the ground. He landed on his side and instantly curled up into a fetal ball, and he didn't really cough so much as just vomited blood from out of his open mouth. But his body was wracked with spasms, so I think now, my boys, that he was not really coughing anymore, no, truly he was gasping just to breathe. But I couldn't hear him over the cries and shouts for the King and the General. The fever of the crowd itself, it buried the sound of his lurching cough."

"Was he all right?" Robbie blurted out.

Burton looked at him, with an arched eyebrow, measuring I guess how much to say to one so little. Then he just said, "No, caro piccolo, he was not." Then Jack Burton looked over at me, to see how I was taking it all in. The arch in his eyebrow disappeared, and his face went strangely blank then. "He was not," he repeated. Not really speaking to me.

"It was dark, even under the lanterns, and from somewhere two or three men and this old woman gathered around us. I discovered I was kneeling bedside my Zio, with both my hands on his shoulders." Burton held his hands out from his lap, and I could almost see that he was holding something gently in his grasp. "I tried to stop the lurching and the trembling in him. But I couldn't. None of us could hear anything over the chanting of the crowd. So with simple gestures that took command of the moment, the old woman had my Ciccio lifted up and carried away, and someone put his arm around me and led me too, along behind.

"I don't remember how, but somehow from the midst of that cheering crowd, the old lady took us to a little stone house, a few narrow streets up from the docks, and they laid my Zio in a bed. And again, I suppose, there was soup and strong, fortified wine. But now, too, there were blankets. Heavy, woolen blankets. For my Ciccio, when he stopped coughing and gasping from exhaustion, and he would collapse into some form of fevered sleep, before long he would be awakened by his own cold shivering. The fever had him freezing and quaking in the warm July night. And then the trembling would start all over again, until he was exhausted, and he collapsed again into brief sleep. If indeed it was sleep.

"You see, it was a sleepless night for me too, as I held my Zio by the shoulders, or I cradled his head in my hands and mopped the sweat from his brow, or I soaked up the blood and spittle and sputum that come from his lungs. His eyes were lost and distant all of that night, and he didn't not know who I was or where he was. I don't think he did, at any rate, but there was no way to tell. He had not the strength to speak, even in his rare calm moments of rest.

"And so it went through that night, now and again interrupted by the old woman, bearing wine or broth or a clean, cool towel. When daylight came, I'd fallen asleep in the morning light, because my Zio had so exhausted himself that he had, I supposed, just passed out.

"I was awakened from my short rest by the old woman leading the General into the room. I know what day it was, too, my boys. I'll always remember the date. It was the Fourth of July."

"The Fourth of July," I said, startled. Jack Burton had taken me far, far away from Independence Day celebrations, so just the sound of that holiday seemed to come at us from a foreign world.

"You knew it, because there were hot dogs and rides and fireworks, didn't you, sir?" said Robbie, and his legs squirmed up under his butt, and Robbie bounced up to attention. It made even me, as green as I was to the world, aware of just how young and foolish my little brother was.

Burton only chuckled a little. He reached back and stroked the black fur tufted on Butto Sammy's crown, and the great ape snorted a little recognition at the touch, and then settled back sleepily on his stool, his black eyelids heavy and drooping. "No," said Jack Burton, and his heart seemed to lighten for a moment. "No, ragazzi, This was not in America. There were no fireworks or carnival rides that day.

"And I wasn't thinking of it that morning, because I didn't know then what that day meant. But now, because of that day, and what happened on the next, I will always remember. See, when you Americans shoot off your fireworks and march your brass bands around, and wave the stars and stripes, I always remember those few days in Genova.

"It was the last time il Generale and Anzani met, and I found out later, it was the birthday of the General. But more than that, when you Americans play your anthems and shoot the skies full of fire, I always remember it as the day they spoke their last to one another. And oh," he paused to take a sharp breath, even after all the years, "the things they said to one another."

He stopped there, and he swallowed hard, and then his head fell forward into his hands, and Jack Burton looked at no one for a long while.

Butto Sammy awakened from his napping, grunted and moved toward Burton. The mountain gorilla bumped him then, gently but surely, with a thick, long forearm. But even that didn't initially rouse the old man in the wheel chair. Butto Sammy looked all around the tent, and he shifted his weight from one front paw to the other, slowly back and forth. And his quiet snorts grew a little sharper, and then a little louder. Finally, after a moment or two of this, he stood up from his stool, and now the ape gave Jack Burton another bump roughly with his shoulder against the old man's shoulder.

Burton jerked up in his wheel chair, his eyes were hard and steely, and with his fists now clenched in his lap, he shouted loudly at the gorilla. "Sit, Butto,' he fairly yelled at the animal. "Down."

I know I sunk a little lower to the ground, to keep out of the way of whatever was coming, and Robbie jumped and shifted back and away from the wheelchair.

"Down!" Burton said, loudly, but not in a shout now. Butto Sammy snorted in defiance, but he did sit back on his little stool. His eyes drooped again and the mountain gorilla seemed calm and content once more. He had achieved what he had set out to do.

Burton cast his head down in his hands again, for a moment, and muttered something in Italian I couldn't make out. Then he sat up and stared at us, at Robbie and me, with the fire gone in his eyes replaced by an old and lingering hurt. He said quietly, "I haven't talked about this, not to anyone, in seventy or eighty years."   It wasn't really meant as an apology, he was just thinking out loud.

But it set me to wondering again just how old this man was. It is a wondering that goes on in me to this very day.

"At the sight of il Generale, my Ciccio sat up in his bed.   It was the strongest I'd seen him look since he collapsed at the dock the day before.   'Francesco,' the General said. Ciccio smiled at him. He seemed better than he had in the hours and hours of the night.

"Then the General looked over at me, and said, 'Comrade Burtoni, I thought we had an understanding. I believe I gave you some orders.'

Before I could answer, my Zio said, 'But you didn't give me any orders, Peppino. You were rying to leave me behind, you were.' My Zio winked at me. 'So don't blame the boy, Peppino. He's a good lad. But not good enough to keep Francesco Anzani out of the action.'   Then Ciccio laughed, but it turned into a burst of coughing that went out of control. And both the General and I had our hands on him then, trying to hold him still, as he shook and shook and shook, trying to get hold of his breath.

"As Ciccio slowly settled back into the bed, the General cut me a look over his shoulder. He didn't have to say anything, because I understood in a moment that I had failed him. This is what I was trying to prevent, is what the General's eyes said. This is who you have failed when you chose not to follow my orders.

"Lying on his side. Ciccio said, once he could get his breath, 'We beat you here to Genova anyway, Peppino. What happened to you?'

"This brought to the General a great laugh. 'Ahh, Francesco,' he said through his great rolling laughter, 'what am I going to do with you?' He ran a hand through his long fair locks, pushing the reddish blonde hair back from his brow. It was the only sign of how worried he was, as he laughed boisterously all the while.

"Then he looked up from under his brow, and he spoke very seriously. 'I want you to stay here, Francesco.' Then his gaze shot over at me, and he said, 'And I want you to stay here with him, Burtoni, until Francesco is strong enough to join us.' His eyes told me this last part was a lie that we both understood. Francesco Anzani was going nowhere. But I nodded yes anyway.

"'Sir,' I snapped back, to affirm his clear orders. Then I added, trying to lie as well as the General, but maybe too I was still young enough to believe in what I said. 'We'll join you in a week or two.'

"Ciccio sat listening to us, seeing straight through it all. 'Where are you headed, Peppino?' he asked, with a steady gaze at the General. It was the only thing Ciccio had left that was steady.

"'I'm taking the Legion,' he answered.

"'The Italian Legion,' Ciccio interrupted him.

116

"The General cracked a little smile, ' I'm taking the Italian Legion to Roverbella, to the front line, to join in the rebellion.'

"Ciccio nodded, and whispered 'Viva Italia!' in a tortured breath, trying to fight off another spasm. In a moment, when he had regained control of himself, he asked, "Who is there, my General?"

"At first il Generale just ignored his question. 'We now have 169 men in the Legion, Francesco. A hundred more have joined us here in Genova.'

"'But who is in Roverbella?' Ciccio pressed his point, his suspicions were high.

"'An army of 96,000 men, Francesco, arrayed against the Austrians. Ready to throw them out of Italia, our Italia, to unite behind the rebels of Milano and Venezia and to free the north of the Austrian tyranny.'

"Ciccio frowned, he stopped and rubbed agitatedly at his forehead as if a headache had struck him suddenly. 'And who is at the head, Peppino, of this army of thousands that the Italian Legion will join? Who will they give their allegiance and their very lives over to, Giuseppe?'

"The General didn't answer. His feet shuffled on the floor, but then he planted them firmly.

"'Who, Giuseppe?' Ciccio said. I had never heard him call the General by that, but the sound of that full first name in the air changed the whole tone of the moment. 'Will it be you, Giuseppe, my General, at the head of that mighty liberating army?'

"'The King of Sardinia is in command," The General said, clearly, if not proudly.

"'Carlo Alberto?' my Ciccio spat out like it was a curse. The General stood still, and did not respond. There was no need to respond.

"'Our Italian Legion, Giuseppe, the heroes of Montevideo, joining the army of the King of Sardinia? Joining the King!'

"'Francesco, you know the old saying, my comrade. You must first catch the hare, before you worry about what sauce to cook it in.'

"'But this hare, Giuseppe . . . No. This King of yours, my General, he may just have the sauce ready for you.'

"'It will not be like that, Francesco.'

"'He will cook you and our whole Italian Legion. Little Peppino, served up on a pretty Sardinian platter for the Austrian's pleasure. And when they are done with you, Giuseppe, I ask you, what will you have? Even if you survive this little feast between these Kings. What will you have left?'

"'We will have an Italia free of the Austrian hussars,' the General said, and he seemed even more planted and square than before.

"'No, Giuseppe, you will have a string of graves scattered for miles and miles around the . . .' Ciccio paused there, and then he spat out again the next few words, "the Kingdom of Sardinia.'

"'No, Francesco, you are wrong.'

"My Zio rose up in the bed, and held himself steady. It was amazing to see, for he truly had not the strength to do it. 'He will use you, my General, and use the whole Legion too, and then he'll make fools of you all. He knows your little proverb about your rabbit stew, Peppino. Kings are always Kings. They don't change because we strolled in wearing our red shirts and toting along a sack of words and dreams.' Ciccio had to stop then, because he did not have the wind to say more, and he would suddenly collapse weakly into coughing if he tried to go further.

"The General took the chance to speak, 'You're wrong, Francesco. It is the first step to our Liberty. You'll see.'

"'No, Peppino,' my Zio said. 'You're just another fool for some other king.' He fell back onto his bed then, and all the glow and the hope from just moments before was gone. 'Leave me alone,' he wheezed.

"'Francesco,' the General said.

"'Get out of my sight,' Ciccio whispered between racked breaths, and he turned away from us.

"The General brought his shoulders up even straighter, and then he barked out, "Captain Francesco Anzani.'

"'Out, fool,' was all Ciccio could say, his head still turned away. 'Fool of Kings. And General of Fools.'

Il Generale drew in a great breath, and his chin pulled in toward his swelled chest. 'You will see, Captain Anzani,' he said.

"'The fool of Kings,' my Ciccio said again, curled on his side and facing away from the General and me. Then he rolled over, and used his last bit of strength to say, 'Get out. Both of you.'

"The General glanced over at me, and his mouth opened to speak an answer, but then his eyes hardened, and with a sharp click of his heels, he just turned and left the room.

"I looked at my Ciccio, and I said, 'Zio?' but he just kept his back toward me, and didn't speak.

"So I honored his wishes, and I left him alone and I followed the General outside. I found him stopped, standing in the cobbled street, his hands behind his back, his head lowered and his back to the door of the little house where my Ciccio lay. That great chest of his was no longer swelled, and he was so lost in thought he didn't notice me behind him, in the doorway to the old lady's house. But I was there, and I heard his whisper. 'Addio, Francesco,' he said. And then more softly, 'Caro Francesco.' And then his head rose straight. And without even a glance backward, he strode away toward the docks, and his ship the Speranza, and to the men of his growing Legion."

"That night, my Zio spent in delirium. He slept little, but he tossed and turned, and in his shouts and cries he seemed to fight every war over again, from Greece to Spain to Uruguay, the battles raged all inside of him again. When the dawn came, I found I'd been up most of the night without any sleep. My eyes burned and I ached in my neck and shoulders, but I had gotten beyond weariness. I felt, ragazzi, like I would never sleep again. Never, never, no never again. No rest. Ever.

"With the daylight, my Ciccio came around, and suddenly his eyes were bright and calm and filled with a new and peaceful clarity. He wasn't able to get up out of his bed, but old Angelina brought us some soft yellow polenta, cooked in chicken broth, and we ate it together. That warm corn meal slipped into me, as I gobbled it down, and I felt life flowing back. And my Zio too, he seemed to grow stronger and his eyes came out of the deep shadows of his brow.

"'Bring me my bag,' Ciccio said, and from the foot of the bed I got the canvas sack that he'd hauled all the way from South America. Sitting up, he dug around in the bag, and out of it, quickly, as he knew just where it was, he pulled out his red blouse. He shook it loose and looked at it, and the he folded it carefully in his lap. Then, very simply, he handed it over to me.

"'Take this to him, Jack Burton,' he said, and the sound of my whole name seemed ominous on his lips.

"'But, I should stay here, 'till you are well,' I protested.

"'No, Peppino is wrong, Gianni. He is making a terrible mistake. And when he discovers this, when he realizes I was right to warn him against this King of his, he will need to know that we are comrades still.' Ciccio shoved the blouse over into my arms. 'Whatever happens to me,' he said. Then he gave me orders again, and again he used my full name. 'Take this to him, Jack Burton. It is the most important thing that you can do now.'

"'But my orders are to stay here with you, my Zio,' I said.

"Ciccio grinned at me, seemed almost fatherly, and then he said, with no little pride, 'I'm giving you your orders now, il piccolo, not our poor mistaken Generale. Not now.' And that lighter tone, and that il piccolo told me all arguments were over.

"Still, I could see a way, I thought, to follow both sets of orders, to follow both my General and my dear Zio, at once.

"'Go. Get some rest, before you leave,' my Zio said, and I had no idea then what he was up to.

"I stood, and turned to head out of the little room, through the same door the General had strode the night before. But I knew I was not leaving. With the red blouse tucked under my arm, I would be back after a few hours of sleep, and I would wait my Ciccio out.

"When I reached the door, and opened it, I heard my Zio speak to me. I turned back, and found he had slumped back down low in the bed. He was breathing shallowly, and he said it again to me. 'Ho un cuore che troppo sente,' he said, though I could barely hear him.

"How could I know those quiet, soft words would be the last words I heard him speak? How could I know?"

Burton sat still in his wheelchair, and the red shirt rested on his little chest behind him, like a lamp now in the darkening tent.

"How could I know?" he muttered again.

"What does it mean?" I said, and I chanted out a few of the sounds, "'Oh quarry . . . what does it mean?"

Burton didn't seem startled by the question, even if he'd seemed distracted moments before. A soft little smile graced his lips.

"I have a heart that feels too much," he said. And then he repeated, "How could I know?"

"Is that the red shirt, right there?" Robbie piped up. "Is that Ciccio's shirt?" He pointed at it, and it seemed to us to glow with legendary fire.

Burton smiled at us, but only for a moment. He reached over again and he put a hand on that red blouse, and he laughed a strange, interrupted laugh. "No," he said. "I gave that shirt to the General, just the way Francesco wanted. This one is my shirt," he said, filled with proud determination.

Jack Burton quietly lifted up the bottle at his feet then, and he took a long draught. But before he drank, he held the bottle up to the heavens, and he said, "Cuore mio" out loud. Then he wiped his mouth on his sleeve, and looked at us, at Robbie and me sitting up straight on the floor.

"It's getting late, lads. Shouldn't you be heading for home?"

"Home!" Robbie cried, and pulled that leaden knapsack over to him. "We left there," he announced, in no uncertain tones.

Burton shook his head, and he was about to tell us that we were not going anywhere with him. But he paused, and seemed to think better of it.

"What happened to Francesco?" Robbie demanded, but I was just quiet, hoping to keep the night going on a little further.

Burton nodded his gray head, and he corked the bottle up and then set it on the ground beside him. "All right then, my little wayfarers," he said, and laughed broadly, but not at us.

He leaned forward out of the wheelchair again, and now he told us the rest of his tale, or as much of it as he was going to tell us, straight away and without a break. From that point, his arms waved in the air, and his voice rose and fell, and he practiced all his charms on us. The lethargy of the smoke was gone. The rest of the story rolled out of him in one great gust, storming over us like a high tide in the wind, relentless and enchanting, until its end. There was no looking back and no longing for voices, for past arms. It was all of a piece. And now it was ours, shared at a run.

"I thought I could follow them both, boys, I would stall and wait for my Ciccio to get stronger, and then I would ride off on some stolen horse to find the General and deliver the red shirt to him. I would tell him Ciccio was well now and waiting, as he rode at the front of the 96,000, raising a country up out of the oppressed lands before them. Everyone's orders would be followed, and everyone was well.

"What did I know? I was younger then. Dreams seemed easy and reachable, and the world in that moment seemed just and fair.

"But what did I know?

"I slept hard for several hours, just blanked out with no memory, dead to all and every sensation, dreamless. It was as if I blinked, as if I just closed my eyes and opened them. But in that flash, hours and hours passed away. I cannot say how long.

"But it was old Angelina's hand that roused me. 'Burtoni,' she said, using the name the General had called me. 'Presto, Burtoni,' she said, 'Presto.' Then she led me down a hallway, so dark I could barely see her black draped form, and then into my Ciccio's candlelit room. I followed her shadow across the darkness, slowly piecing together my sense of who I was and where we were.

"His bed clothes were soaked, and his color was simultaneously burning red and a bloodless white. 'Ciccio,' I said, and took his hand. He looked over at me, but he didn't see me. 'Blanco' he muttered. And then he shouted 'Gomez.' His head lolled back and forth, and in his eyes he saw, I know now, the great retreat from Salto. 'Water,' he called for, 'Giuseppe, water. Acqua.'

"Angelina brought him a cup, and the both of us tried to get him to drink, but he wouldn't take it. He'd just turn his burning head aside, and call out again for 'Water!'

"When I told the General about these last minutes, and about the strange words Ciccio cried out, the General just nodded his head and explained it to me.

"'He was living again our great defeat at San Antonio, il piccolo,' the General told me. 'We retreated under fire to Salto, but for a day and a half, under the burning Uruguayan sun, little Burtoni, we were penned down by the forces of Gomez's Blancos. Pinned down, in full dress and arms, under that huge hot sun, without a drop of water to be had. Gomez thought he had us then, with the sun and the heat at his side, but we fought so bravely, and how we suffered, until we won our retreat back to the safety of Salto, and the waters of the Rio Uruguay. To that sweet water. Never has there been any sweeter, il piccolo. Never. But Francesco, my dear Anzani, he was living it all over again. Those long hours under that torrid sun.'

"But it was only a little while that my Ciccio called out for his General, and he never really came around. His head tossed back and forth weakly for a while, and then it came to its rest, turned away from us. Old Angelina crossed herself, and she leaned past me to close his eyes, and turn his head back to rest gently. And he was gone. Gone to that great rest that waits for all of us. Some of us too soon, like my dear Zio. Francesco Anzani, gone before he'd seen forty years. And for some of us, it seems never to come. We just go on and on, growing older and feebler, suffering more and more, and all the more and more alone.

"Angelina took me away from him, then. There was no more for us to do, and life needed to go on. She fed me in silence at a table in her tiny kitchen, a thick and grainy soup, filled with beets and parsnips and other roots from down in the earth.

"It was there, eating silently, waiting for the undertaker to come and remove my dear Zio, that I understood. Ciccio had known exactly what he was doing. I was free now to follow all my orders, to follow both the General, and my Zio.

"You see, Ciccio was sending me away. He was setting me free, and at the same time charging me to find Il Generale, to deliver the red shirt, and to save him. This was what he had ordered me to do. Not to linger around, worrying over his remains. That was of no importance to him.

"What was of import to my Ciccio was the General, that is, to save the General from his own mistakes. This was the most important thing I could do now. And at last I understood it.

"And so, my boys, I left my dear Anzani in the care of old Angelina, and right that moment I set out on the trail of il Generale. I took only my few things, and my Ciccio's red shirt, and with his last real words echoing in my ears all the way, I set out on foot for Roverbella, where the General and his legion had gone a day ahead of me.

"I walked across the short plain and then up into the mountains, the Apennines that hung down to the coast there in Liguria. But as I strode along, I realized how far I had to go. The Legion was ahead of me, but they were rested from their days in Nice, and from the long wandering voyage to Genova. They were marching east across the mountains toward Mantova and the Romagna at double pace, with the General and Aguiar at their head, the heroes of Italia. The General on his white charger, and Aguiar the batman right at his side.

"But I was trudging along, alone, armed with only Ciccio's pack on my back, and with days and days of spotty food and sleepless nights caring for my Zio behind me. My Ciccio, now dead and gone. It was not long, only a mile or two into my march to the Apennines, before I realized how worn and tired I truly was, and how rugged the way ahead lay over the mountains. And so I fell far behind the Legion, and I stopped to sleep in the summer woodlands, and along the way the good Ligurian liberals would feed me, and point me the way that our Legion had gone on ahead.

"You see, I was following in the wake of the good will of Il Generale and his march, and I benefited time and again from the Manzinians along the way, who fed me and put me up, and told me which towns were filled with the priests and the sympathizers of the Austrians and their Croat mercenaries, the Ligurian patriots told me which places to avoid or to pass through quietly, and at night. And where I could not go safely. Still my pace was too slow and circuitous, for I was one and not a Legion of hundreds marching through.

"And along the way, as I climbed up over the Apennines and the down into the wide valley of the Po, into Emilia Romagna and the Veneto, the news of the General and his men kept filtering back to me, traveling from tongue to tongue, the tales of his fate at Roverbella and beyond. And with every piece of news, it became clear how far my Zio Ciccio had seen into the future. Francesco Anzani had understood something about kings and their ilk that the General, great as he was, could not see. He was too trusting a nature, il Generale. So my Ciccio was right, after all, and he'd sent me off not on some wild hunt, but for a reason. I was to save the General from himself. This was my charge, from the deathbed of my Ciccio.

"You see, little ragazzi, when the General and his Legion arrived, ready to lead the charge against the Austrians, King Carlo Alberto already had other ideas. This King was a sharp one, lads, sharp enough to realize that a revolutionary like il Generale was more dangerous to him than the Austrians were. With an army of 96,000 at his beck and call, what did he need from a rebel and a couple hundred of his veteran followers? Noting at all. Nothing, lads, that's what.

"So by the time I crossed the pass and reached Bobbio, the word had already traveled back to Liguria, and to me. The king had turned the Italian Legion away. He'd sent the General and his men away to the War Office, back in Torino. Far, far away from the front lines. Hundreds of miles from the front line, from the ensuing battle.

"And so from Bobbio I turned to head off to the north, toward Milano, thinking I might cut the triangle and catch up with the Legion on their march to the west.   This hope lifted my spirits, and I picked up my pace, but I only arrived in Milano to hear the news.   The General had stopped there, and appealed to the provisional government of the new Lombardia. 'Give me a post, so that we, the Italian Legion, can fight the Austrians. We will fight for Lombardia, if the Sardinians have no use for us.'

"But, before I was even half way to the outskirts of Milano, the General and his men had pressed on for Torino. He'd gone on to report to the War Office, as ordered by the King. And the word on the streets of Alessandria was that Mazzini had spoken for him, but the Lombards too were afraid of this wild, fair-haired South American General from Nizza.

"So I headed after them west toward Torino, across the valleys and the plain of the Po again.   But Francesco Anzani had been right. When the General arrived at the Sardinian War Office, they'd already heard from their King. They too had no use for the Legion, even 200 miles behind the front lines. They told the General to go and try to help in the Veneto, to go to Venice and become a privateer in the Adriatic and defend the Venetian Republic. In other words, ragazzi, they all told the General to go and get lost.

"So the General and the Legion turned back for Milano, where Mazzini had been pleading his case. When I arrived in Torino I learned that the Legion had been sent further north, to Bergamo, where the General and his men were put safely to work training the army's reinforcements.

"But I was exhausted by my journey then, and at times I despaired of ever catching up with the men of the Legion, as they were bounced around the foot of the Alps like a child's ball. But in time, I found a friend of my Ciccio's, one Danielle who had fought with him in Greece, though now an old man of 80. I stayed with him there, sleeping in a bed at night and eating hardy during the day, thanks to Danielle's love for our dear departed Anzani. It crossed my mind to find some work there in Torino, and maybe make this fine town my home at last, because I had grown weary in heart and body of chasing after the General. He was being run and run around the countryside, with every leader of every stretch of a little land afraid of him.

"Yet I knew, O lads, once I'd rested that Francesco Anzani's scarlet shirt was still in my pack. And I knew, more than ever, that my Ciccio was right, and he'd sent me on a mission to save his old comrade, and in saving him, to save our mutual cause. To be true, it was Danielle who stirred me to go on. For he understood in his old age, the importance of the wishes of a dying man. And the importance, too, of true friends.

"And so one morning, with the summer sun already rising high, and with the Alps ahead of me. I waved goodbye to Danielle and I set off again to the north. This time I would catch up with them in Bergamo."

"But a strange thing happened then, lads. As I pressed on, walking the dirt roads on foot, to Bergamo, the news of what was happening in the fields of that summer began to filter back to me, piecemeal, at my every stop along the way. You see, the damned Austrians under Radetzky defeated the great army of the 96,000. He whipped them like they were scared children, in a big empty field near Custozza. Radetsky routed them, he did, and sent them off at a run in every direction. And then he marched on toward Milano, to seize back that rebellious city.

"Suddenly, the grand Republic of Milano was lost in pure terror, sure that the city and its revolution would be ransacked by the angry Austrian forces and their lean and hungry Croat mercenaries. The new Republic of Milano just folded up and died, and in their panic they began to evacuate the city.

"It was in a little hollow, a day or two's walk from Bergamo, that I came upon a fire burning under an old oak tree, and I met two of the fleeing soldiers of Carlo Alberto, escapees from the battle of Custozza. One was named Paolo and the other Umberto, and they were so young they seemed only a little older than me. Of course, it wasn't true. Lads, it only seemed that way. I had decades of age on them, even if they couldn't see it.

"I joined their fireside, and they shared with me some of the two rabbits they were roasting there on a spit made of sticks. And they told me, as only young men still charged with the excitement of battle can talk, about their frightful defeat at Custozza. Of the way the fearsome Croats in stark white uniforms marched out in such tight formation they seemed like blades of ice, and they mowed across the campo slicing through the Sardinian lines despite the superior numbers on our side. And oh, how every single one of the 96,000 was turned and then fled before that white, bayoneted precision, flashing across the grass.

"And then, with my hands greasy from the hare I was eating, it was Paolo who said the words that nearly made me choke. 'But those damned Croats have yet to meet the Anzani Brigade,' he said. I nearly dropped the hare's leg in my lap.

"'The who?' I said.

"Umberto nodded his black hair, all mussed and standing up in the air, and said, 'From Milano, they've sent out a small band of soldiers, all dressed in Red tunics, to harass the goddamned Austrians on their push toward the city. And they will do it, by God.'

"'The Anzani Brigade,' Paolo said, his mouth full of rabbit.

"'Who leads this brigade?' I asked. 'How many are there?'

"'It's only a few hundred men,' Paolo said, and then he wiped his mouth on his jacket sleeve. 'Every one of them in bright red.'

"'And who leads them?' I repeated.

"The two lads shrugged, but I was sure this was my General. I wiped the grease from my hands on my pants, and then on the grass, and got them as clean as I could, and then I carefully pulled out my Zio's shirt, folded in the bottom of the pack. 'This is Anzani's shirt,' I said, holding up the red blouse for them both to see.

"Their eyes grew big and I told them who Francesco was, and how he died, and who I was searching for. 'It's him,' I said. 'It must be him.'

"'It must be him,' repeated Umberto.

"And so that was it, ragazzi. In the morning we rose at first light, and the three of us together set out to find the Anzani Brigade."

Robbie popped up unto his knees and shouted out, "Anzani!" It made Jack Burton laugh, and then we all laughed together.

Robbie looked over his shoulder at me, and with burning eyes, he whispered to me, 'The Anzani Brigade! That will be our name, Will." Then his round head shot back around to Burton. "Did you find them, sir?"

*   *   *

Burton sat up a little straighter in his chair now, and he licked his lips once or twice, as if he was tasting that old spit roasted hare from long ago, but it may have been just the long, long tale he was telling. "We did not find il Generale at first. He was moving faster than we were, and the country was changing right under our feet.

"But Paolo, Umberto and I, we were moving more quickly now, lads. We had just two smooth bore muskets with us, and they were still wearing their sky blue uniforms. So along the way back toward Milano, we met many, many folk ready to feed us or to offer us a ride. But as we grew closer to the city, the crowds began to change. Suddenly people were fleeing, and when we asked them if they'd heard where the Anzani Brigade was last seen, they all just pointed to the north, to the north and then they hurried on to the south.

"Then one day, as we reached the outskirts of the city, a gray bearded man with a donkey cart full of wine casks waved us over to him on the road. 'You boys,' he warned us, 'Ragazzi miei, take off those jackets and lose them. And hide those muskets somewhere too.' His eyes were staring wide, and he shot glances all around us at the bustling roadway, filled with people pressing their way out of the city, carrying whatever they could on their backs and in hand carts or dog carts or anything that would move.

"It was he that told us the news. Carlo Alberto had surrendered."

"No," Robbie and I said in the same breath.

Burton just nodded his head, sagely it seemed to us. "The war was over, lads. The dream of Italia was dead and gone again. And my General, he was now an outlaw. So much for the brave hearts of Kings, O ragazzi."

"Ciccio was right," snarled Robbie, and he seemed truly crestfallen. His little hand lay limp and still on his lunken pack.

"Still, all was not lost to the treachery and cowardice of the King, lads. No, you see, the General had turned the Brigade northward again, and his plan was to head up into the lake country there, and the Brigade would fight a guerilla war, just as he had done in Montevideo and in Rio Del Sol. The Anzani Brigade would fight, harassing the enemy from the mountains around the lakes, and then slipping off into the safety of Switzerland when they needed to rest.

"Radetzky and his Hessians pushed after the Brigade, passing through fallen Milano without a fight. Paolo, Umberto and I, trying as we were to catch up with the Brigade, we wound up in the countryside around Varese, between the slow advancing Austrian horde and the swiftly moving General and his cohorts. He and his men were moving so quickly about, it seemed for a long while hopeless that we could ever catch up with them.

"Then one night, by a little pond in the Varesotto, the three of us were resting by our fire, eating a duck we had taken from the pond, when someone approached us out of the dark. Umberto seized his gun, and rose up onto his feet. 'Show yourself,' he commanded into the dark around us.

"Then I heard my name. 'Bur-Burtoni?' the voice said, but I didn't recognize it.

"'Who are you?' I said, and a man emerged out of the dark with his hands up. 'How do you know me?' I said to him, for I swear I had never seen him before.

"Paolo too now had his musket unshouldered and pointed at the stranger. 'I don't know you,' I said to the scruffy man who emerged into the firelight.

"'I wa-was with the Ge-General,' the stranger stuttered, out of fear I thought, but I was wrong.

"'I don't remember you, signore,' I said. 'You were not on the Speranza.'

"'N-No,' he shook his head, and started to lower his arms.

"'Keep them up,' snarled Umberto.

"'No,' he jerked his hands back up in the air, his stutter disappearing for a moment in fear, and he stepped forward until I could see him more clearly in the firelight. He was unkempt and ragged, in just his shirtsleeves, though the summer night at the foot of the Alps was cool. 'I wa-was in Ni-Ni-Nizza,' he said, his Italian accent florid with French, even through his ragged stutter. "I ja-joined the Bri-Bri-Brigade there. And it was the-there I saw-saw you, with Fran-Fran-Francesco Anzani, and the-the General's mother, Bur-Bur-Bur-Burtoni. You don-don't know me, but I know-know you.'

"I realized there were not many who would recognize me as the lad who'd stayed with Ciccio there at the house of the General's mother. So he had to be someone who was with us, at least from the landing at Genova. 'Sit down,' I said, and nodded him toward the fire. Paolo and Umberto slowly lowered their arms, still not quite sure of the stuttering stranger. We gave him some of the duck we had taken from the pond, and he sat and ate hungrily.

"And then he told us, in his broken way, where the brigade was and how it was fairing. When the news of the King's surrender came to the Brigade, the stuttering soldier said, there was great dissension in the ranks. You see, more than half of them understood that to fight on was fruitless. The Austrians with their ruthless Croatian mercenaries had won, taking everything at Custozza, and then Milano and most of the Veneto had fallen, with Venice herself surely soon to follow. Still, despite the armistice Carlo Alberto had signed, our General decided to continue his fight as long as he could.

"After that, some of the Brigadiers began to slip away every night, and before long fighting broke out amongst the men. Those who were loyal to the dreams of the General tried to hold the deserters, to call out the traitors and threaten them. But this led only to a real danger of mutiny, and the General understood that.

"So it went, until one night at Castelleto, the General brought everyone together. 'Almost a th-thousand men,' said the stuttering Brigadier. And there the General announced his plans. He had written a document. It was a manifesto, and he read from it for those of us who couldn't read. So our little stuttering Brigadier then he pulled out three or four sheets of a broadside, they were folded up and tucked inside his pocket. He handed one of them over to us.

"This is the drift of what it said, boys.

"Il Generale, with his great heart, lads, he announced to the assembled men that those who wanted to go, who wanted to give in to the foreigners' domination of our country, they were free to go. He would not have Legionnaires spilling the blood of other Legionnaires. So there would be no fighting amongst the men, and no one would stop those who chose to leave. But only on one condition could they desert so freely. And at that, he set a stack of handbills on the ground and said, 'If you desert us now, at least take these and post them in every town and village, wherever you go. Abandon your red shirt, but take instead all you dare to carry of these, and let the word get out that not everyone is so weak as our so-called King.'

"Umberto and I snatched the 'Castellato Manifesto' up as greedily as that little Brigadier had eaten his duck just moments before. And as we read the General's proclamation that the war of independence was not yet over for him, the stuttering soldier told us more.

"Over half of the Anzani Brigade deserted peacefully that night. And maybe only half of those fleeing the Brigade had the courage to take copies of the Manifesto with them. By daylight the Anzani Brigade was only a hundred men or so again, and the General marched them along the River Ticino toward Lago Maggiore. We were down, now, to the true and great men of the Speranza. And we were a Legion again. We were the core of the Anzani Brigade now, we were the Anzani Legion. And we would stand by him always.

"The other thing the stuttering soldier told us was what the General planned to do. With what was left of the Brigade, with his Anzani Legion, he seized the town of Arona on the shores of Lago Maggiore, and from there he commandeered two little steamships, the Verbano and the San Carlo, built to haul rich Swiss tourists around the lake. So the General was on the water again, a sailor once more, where he always felt most at home.

"At dawn we left the stuttering soldier asleep by the ashes of our dead fire, and we headed to the north and the west, pressing toward the General's base, Arona. But in my heart I knew that the Anzani Legion with its two ships on that great lake would be hard for us to catch. They would be moving quickly, from the western shore to the eastern shore, raiding the Austrian forces quickly, and then disappearing just as they had appeared. And they would be almost impossible, without a touch of dumb luck, for three young lads on foot to find. Not to mention that there were dangers, lads, for us in asking after the two ships. We couldn't just question anyone. Many, many along the way favored the Austrians, or feared them. And it would do me no good to find myself locked up with Paolo and Umberto under some Croat guard, with the red shirt of Francesco Anzani certainly seized and destroyed. That would be no way to fulfill my Zio's last wish.

"So, it was with high hopes, lads, but little in the way of a plan that we marched off deeper into the lake country. We moved, naturally, toward Arona, though the chances that the Verbano and the San Carlo would put in there were slim. The Legion could not as yet defend a home, so it could indeed not have one. Still, Arona seemed the place to start searching for Il Generale and his men.

"That sunny afternoon, on a dirt road headed west, Paolo spilled out of his bag a little three button bandoneon. As we walked along, our bellies full, with Umberto's and Paolo's young hopes high, Paolo shouldered his rifle and started to play a dancing tune on his little squeezebox. 'This is my home country,' he said happily.

"Umberto laughed at him. 'We're walking away from there, Paolo,' he said.

"'Well, back there in the Val d'Arno,' he said anyway. 'We're close to my home.'

"'To our home, but were still walking away from it,' Umberto said. Then suddenly, he started to sing to the melody of the bandoneon. They were nonsense syllables, just musical noise, but he followed along with the tune on the little instrument, and surely it was an old country tune from deep in those boys' homeland. It wasn't very long before I joined in, for the melody was sweet and simple, and easy to follow, and so the three of us strutted down the road toward the great lake, singing as we went."

Robbie laughed and rolled back and forth on his knees in some rhythm he heard in his head. "We can do that too," he shouted. "We can sing as we march along."

Jack Burton grinned at my little brother, but he didn't answer. He looked over at the sleepy-headed ape sitting on the stool behind him, and he whispered to him. "Zambutto," he whispered. "La musica."

That was all Burton needed to say, for then Zambutti Sam rose up on his thick haunches and moved almost soundlessly across the floor, walking on all fours, the knuckles of his curled forepaws carrying him gracefully to the door of the tent, where he slipped out through the canvas and into the dark night outside.

Meanwhile, Jack Burton leaned forward in the wheelchair, and went on with his story as if there'd been no interruption. "One morning, as we were approaching the outskirts of Arona on a dusty and rutted road, Paolo was whistling happily, when suddenly Umberto put a hand on both our shoulders and said, 'Listen!' Once we stood still, and Paolo stopped his little tune, we heard clearly the sound of horses and the clatter of arms. Paolo's eyes grew big, and he whispered, 'Austrians.'

"'Or mercenaries,' hissed Umberto, who with the wave of his hand, led us over into the trees, off the side of the road.

"As we moved deeper into the pines, the sounds of the army marching grew louder. We crept up to a high ledge and peeked over it, down into the vale below us. There lay a wide, sandy carriage road heading toward the lake and Arona, and it was filled with soldiers and cavalry and mules pulling ten or twelve pieces of artillery.

"'The Austrians?' I said. 'Ahead of us.'

"Paolo and Umberto didn't respond. We just laid low on the ground and watched the troops march by, and I realized slowly that these troops were wearing the same sky blue uniforms that my two friends had abandoned back in Milano. Then a little fat man on a black charger sporting a lot of silver brocade rode back from the front of the line and shouted some orders to the men with the artillery mules.

"'The Duke,' whispered Paolo, and glanced over at Umberto. He gave just a short nod, and then Paolo whistled his wide-eyed surprise. Umberto silenced him with a glance.

"So we watched as this army marched on into Arona ahead of us. When they'd passed by our brushy ledge, and were out of earshot, I asked my friends, 'Who are they?'"

At that moment, Zambutto Sammy lifted the tent door and lumbered awkwardly back inside, on three legs. Cradled in his left arm like an infant was a bright red octagonal box, closed with straps of red leather and brass buckles. The ape rose up onto his hind legs and waddled like an old woman across the rug laid out on the ground, and then sat down carefully on his stool, before he leaned forward and handed the red and brass box in his paw over to Jack Burton. It was all done so easily, even if it was done awkwardly, and with only the slightest gestures from Burton to direct the mountain gorilla, who gave out an occasional small snuff and grunt as he clambered over to his place on the stool. I knew that this was not the first time Zambutti Sam had been sent out for the magic red box.

Burton stopped his story then, and laid the box quietly on the rug at his feet. Zambutti Sam settled onto his stool, and the cloud of smoke drew back over his eyes, and he seemed even more content than before. Skillfully, Burton unlatched the brass buckles and unfolded the box, and before our eyes it turned into a little red bandoneon, with worn brass buttons to match the buckles.

Burton slipped his hands through the leather straps and then gently pulled the instrument open. From it streamed a wheezing high chord, not loud but intense. In the next moment we heard the clicking of the buttons and saw Burton's fingers fly, and an old melody ushered out in to the circus night, and filled the tent with the sounds of far away and distant lands beyond broad seas filled with uncertain wayfarers and warriors for long lost causes. The music poured easily into our open ears and then filled our two hearts beating with longing and wanderlust. It was magic, even though it was simple.

Somewhere, in the midst of this forlorn little song, Burton began to speak again, and now he was accompanying his story with the strains of the bandoneon. "This, my boys, this is the little squeeze box that belonged to Paolo, indeed. Whenever I remember he and Umberto and those days, I need to pull this out and play the old tunes he taught me around the fires at night. And the song that he and Umberto sang that day at Arona, it was like this one, as best as I can remember, lads. As best as I can remember." Zambutti Sam sighed loudly, contentedly, and the ape settled over on his side, resting on one of those great long forearms of his, and I saw the beast close his eyes. I think he went to sleep, happy at the sound of Jack Burton's voice, and at the familiar strains of the red and brass bandoneon.

"Who were they?" I asked, still in my mind's eye somewhere on a ledge in the brush above a dirt road that led into Arona, near the shores of Lago Maggiore.

"It was the Duke of Genova, leading an army of that vile surrendered King, Carlo Alberto of Sardinia. This is what Umberto told me, after they had marched on past us and entered Arona.

"But I was confused, lads. 'Why don't we go join them,' I said happy as a fool. We had found our way to the fight at last, I thought. 'They are with us!' I nearly shouted, 'and maybe they know where we can catch up with the General, and the Anzani Legion.'

"Paolo and Umberto looked at one another, and I said to them, "What is it?'

"'Burtoni,' Paolo said, eyes wide. 'We are deserters. You forget.'

"'Oh,' I muttered, and then I was about to object, because after all everyone had deserted from the fields of Custozza.

"But Umberto didn't let me go on. He led us quietly into town, after the troops, and he reminded us that the King had signed an armistice. And he was right, lads, because that night we drank wine at an inn and with the vino came the truth from the soldiers of the Duke. You see, O ragazzi, the Duke had been sent by old Carlo Alberto, who was his brother, to arrest our General, and to bring in the renegades of Anzani, all of them under their new treaty with the Austrians. They were not only cowards, ragazzi, they were traitors. The bunch of them. Traitors. They'd run from the Austrian Hussars, and now they had turned and were marching on their own heroes."

"Did they get him?" said Robbie, sounding a bit breathless.

"Oh, hell no, lads," shouted Burton. "Hell no. The Anzani Legion was long gone ahead of us, and in fact we learned that night of their victory across the Lago to the north. At Luino, just two days before, the Legion had been attacked by a detachment of 700 Croats, and the General and his men had sent them fleeing away, and then they sailed off across the lake with 33 Croat prisoners, besides.

"The word had already traveled back to Arona, and the Duke's soldiers were worried. They were angry at this forced march, and they were angry at the Anzani Legion, roaming wild through the lands around Lago Maggiore. And now, with the word of the Croats' hard defeat, they were afraid of the General and his renegades, too. Traitors, filled with fears.

"So we understood, quickly, that Arona was no place for three young soldiers trying to join up with the Anzani Legion. It was no longer safe to be secreting a red shirt around in your pack, especially one that had belonged to old Francesco Anzani himself, and one that was meant to be given to our General.

"'What do we do now?' said Paolo as we were settling in to sleep on a hillside outside of town, still warmed by the red wine we'd shared with the soldiers of the Duke.

"'We head north, around the lake and then up along the west shores,' I said.

"'Until, somewhere, we can catch up to the Legion,' Paolo said, his teeth shining in the dark from his grin.

"Umberto, sleeping between us, began to snore open mouthed. Umberto was one of those lads who sleeps hard on a bellyful of wine, boys. Paolo gave him a poke in the ribs and it startled him. 'Heah!' he grunted, and then flopped over on his side. 'Get some sleep,' he muttered crankily.

"Paolo's white grin shone on a little longer. 'Buona Notte,' he said, and lay down flat, the wine making him want to talk. 'We'll catch up with them to the north. And then we'll be part of the Anzani Legion.' And he talked some more, but it was to the summer stars, ragazzi, because the wine and the sound of his warm voice chattering on and on, punctuated with the fat snores of Umberto, they carried me sweetly off to sleep."

I let loose with a big yawn, brought on by Burton's story of the sleeping lads, and by the soft wheezing music of Paolo's bandoneon. At the sound of my yawn, Robbie jerked around and stared at me, furiously. He whispered my name, and I nodded my head and sat up straighter. Burton grinned at the two of us, but he never paused in his story. He was back there again himself, enchanted by his own bandoneon playing.

"In the bright dawn we hiked off to the south around the foot of the lake, keeping the waters of Lago Maggiore off to our left almost always in our sight, and with high hopes of at last finding the Legion.

"But they were moving quickly, boys, always a day or so ahead of us, it seemed. It took us two days walking around the lake, before we reached the little town of Algera, and that was where we heard the news. You see, the General had split the Legion in two, because he knew the Duke of Genova was coming at them from the south, and from the northwest the Austrians were marching, a huge army under d'Aspre, to cut off his retreat into Switzerland. He understood that he was caught between their pinchers. So he sent most of the men away, on board their two ships, carrying their prisoners east and south along the lake, and he told them to escape. And when the time was ripe, to be ready to fight.

"And then Il Generale took just 60 of his men and they marched south across the mountains toward Varese. His plan was to be small, to move quickly, and to fight his war in the mountains between Maggiore and Como. I knew these were the men from the Speranza, Aguiar and Captain Gazollo and the others. They were the ones who had the heart of Anzani, beating still in their chests, feeling too much, lads. Feeling too much.

"Umberto looked at Paolo, and he said, 'My friend, we are headed home.' But I didn't understand what they meant.

"'We will catch them there,' Umberto said, with a sharp mod of his head. 'If there is anywhere we can catch up with il Generale, it is there.'

"'We'll take you right to him now,' Paolo said, and skipped a step in the grass as he walked.

"'How can you be so sure?' I said, tired of trudging and feeling the heavy weight of that red shirt stuffed in my pack.

"'Because, Burtoni, we're headed home,' Umberto said, and then Paolo laughed a merry cackle.

"'Home,' he sang, and unpacked this little red bandoneon."

"My two friends hailed from an old medieval town a few miles south of Varese by the Val d'Arno, a village called Morazzone. We reached there in the late afternoon. It was at the end of August. We had spent more than 6 weeks tramping around the countryside between Milano and Torino and Lago Maggiore, living off the good will of strangers and patriots, sleeping under the stars and borrowing a chicken or a rabbit along the way when we needed it, and always with our eyes searching the horizons, gazing off ahead of us into the valleys and behind us on the hillsides, always watching for the foreigner. To put it simply, lads, we were tired. And the sight of the old stone walls and the cobbled streets of Morazzone felt like home to me, so I can only imagine how Paolo and Umberto felt to be home, for true and for real."

Robbie frowned, and he glanced back at me, and over at the napping gorilla. And then he said, protesting quietly, but with a real worry in his voice. "You didn't find them?" he cried incredulously. "You never gave him your Ciccio's shirt?" His outrage overwhelmed his disappointment.

Burton threw his head back and cocked it over to one side, and for a moment he let loose with some wild, dissonant riffs on Paolo's bandoneon, and Zambutto Sammy stirred from his sleep, and then Burton let the instrument wheeze down to a whisper, and without a smile or a laugh, with nary a wink, he said, "As luck would have it, boys, that is where, at long last, we caught up with them." And his cloudy eyes sparkled as he spoke.

Then he settled back in his wheelchair, and he looked at me, straight into my eyes, before he began again to tell his tale to Robbie, and then the gorilla nestled back into his nap.

"As we climbed up toward little Morazzone, nestled on top of a little hill above the valley, we saw some movements in the evening light on the hillside just below the village. So we slowed down, and it was Umberto who, crouching next to us by an old wall, identified them. 'Croats,' he whispered to Paolo and me.

"'Are you sure?' Paolo protested. 'What would they be doing here?' You could tell, Paolo wanted only to go home, at long last.

"'I don't know,' Umberto muttered. 'I can't be sure.'

"And that was when, up in the village, I saw them, clustered here and there in the narrow streets just above us. The Red Shirts. 'It's the General,' I said, searching frantically with my eyes for the long blond locks of his hair stuffed under that scruffy brown hat of his. 'The Legion,' I said, before I was really sure, but pointing anyway, for I could not see the General.

"'It must be their sentries over there, on the lower slope of the hill' said Umberto.

"'It's not the Croats,' said Paolo. 'It is the lookouts of the Anzani Legion, Umberto.' And at that Paolo rose up on his feet and danced up the wooded hillside toward the little village on the crest of the hill.

"Umberto glanced at me, and then shrugged in agreement, and so we followed Paolo up the hill into Morazzone, though I was too tired to do any dancing, and I think, lads, Umberto still sensed that something was not right." Burton let the bandoneon fall suddenly silent. "We should have known we were walking into the opened jaws of a trap."

"Croats," I muttered, involuntarily.

Burton glanced up at me, his eyes wired with sadness. "The Austrian dogs of d'Aspre," he hissed, and the bandoneon snapped closed with a sigh in his lap.

"We should have known. We should have trusted Umberto's instincts. We could have saved many lives that day, including some of our own," Burton said. "But those boys were young, and they were home. Paolo was dreaming of the warm lights of his village, and Umberto loved his friend too well to stop him. Umberto was too young to know how quickly and how hard and unfairly the end can come. And I was so tired of traveling along, in pursuit of some last wish for my dead Zio. I wanted too badly to find the General, and to fulfill Anzani's last wish, that I let the caution of my years slip away. I acted like a boy as young as I looked. So up the hillside we went, sometimes trudging, sometimes dancing, up into the narrow cobbled streets of Morazzone." Burton gazed up then, first at Robbie, and then over at me. "Remember that name, lads," he said

"Morazzone," Robbie replied.

"Morazzone," I said.

"There were old, medieval houses, all stone and many of them three stories tall. And the narrow streets that wound between them were cobbled, most of them mere passages where two men could not pass one another without both of them turning to the side. For long periods of the day, they were so narrow they lay in shadows and so they were mossy and damp from the spray and the fog that rose from the valley of the Arnetto, the little Arno. Paolo, who was lanky and tall, he wandered along the streets, touching the damp walls on either side of him, whistling another tune.

"I followed him and Umberto up through that maze of streets, and wherever we came upon a cart or a donkey or even a friendly dog, we had to press to the side, to one wall or the other to get past. Still Paolo scurried along, skipping like the boy he still was at heart," and here Burton opened the bandoneon and played that lilting tune again. "And in just moments he led us out into a sunny little piazza, with the wooded hills across the valley rising high all around us, and with a little stream trickling down from the center of the village. There was a well there, with a spring fed trickle curling down through an old stone channel into the valley, with stone pools of fresh water along the way. Around the well spring, that little piazza was filled with people, women and children, the villagers, and standing scattered about among them were the men in their Red Shirts, mixing into the old yellow stone of the piazza. And that is where I saw him.

"He was giving out orders to the Legionnaires around him, trying to keep everything together and quiet, but without much luck. And he was arguing, too, with a tall black haired man in boots and a fine leather vest. 'If you don't give it to us,' he said to the scowling man in the vest, 'you will force us to take it, Signore. And we don't want to take it. We don't want to do things that way.'

"'Threats!' shouted out the man in the vest, and he spat on the stones of the piazza, though carefully not messing up his boots. 'And what do we do when the foreigner comes? Huh? Do we feed them too?'

"'Signore, they won't ask first,' said the General, looking past the man and eyeing the rows of hillsides across the valley. 'They'll just take what they need. And then, Signor Podesta, they'll take what they like. And when they are done with that, they'll take some more.'

"Paolo fairly waltzed his way across the square, slipping past the villagers and the Legionnaires like a child in a crowd, and then he strode directly up to the General. 'Signor Antonio, what is the problem?' Paolo said, loudly enough so we could hear it across the piazza.

"This man called Antonio was shocked at first, and then a big grin brightened his scowling face. 'Paolo,' he said, and then seeing us following him across the stones, 'Umberto! You boys are alive!' he cried out.

"That was when the General saw me. 'Burtoni,' he said quietly, and then more loudly, 'Il piccolo.' And while there was no smile, I felt the warm welcome in his eyes. But he and the Legion were hungry, and he was still negotiating.

"It took only moments for the homecoming of Paolo and Umberto to change everything. And soon we were all eating, sitting on the stones of the piazza, jugs of wine, rounds of bread and pieces of roasted chicken appearing as if from nowhere into the hands of the women and children of Morazzone, as they spread it out amongst us, and as Paolo flitted around the piazza with a bucket of spring water from the well and a dipper, from which we all drank happily.'

"Did you give him the red shirt then?" Robbie squirmed on his knees.

Burton smiled sweetly, and said, "Not yet, piccolo mio. Not yet." The old man paused and his eyes rolled up to the ceiling of the tent then, while he gazed at something deep inside himself. Then he took in a deep breath, and it made me wonder again about the smoke, which had filled his head and made Zambutti Sam so sleepy.

"Umberto, good Umberto, he stood there beside the General, his eyes filled with ardor and courage. Oh if you could have seen him, with his great fire. But I heard a deep voice sing out my name just then, and there was Aguiar, sitting on the little bench beside the well, with his hand dangling down near the cool earthy waters. He waved me over, with a chunk of bread and half a chicken grasped in one big hand.

"And so we shared the chicken and a beaker of red wine, and as the food soaked into me, I realized how truly tired I was, how all the wandering and roaming over these hills on foot or sometimes with a borrowed ride on a cart or a wagon, it had all worn me down. How good it felt to sit still in that little piazza centro of Morazzone on those old stones, and to eat with my old comrades from the Speranza. The comrades I thought I might never see again. But it wasn't long before that mood changed, once we were rested and eating, and all the halloos were over, when Aguiar, with his big hand on my shoulder, asked 'You were there when Francesco died, Burtoni?'

"I nodded yes.

"'Tell me,' Aguiar said, 'was it easy? Did our friend die well?'

"I nodded again. 'He died knowing he would be remembered,' I said. 'He died knowing we would carry his struggle onward.'

"'So Francesco died a happy death,' Aguiar said to the clear waters of the well beneath his dusty boots. I didn't need to say anymore, though I felt the weight of my Ciccio's shirt, like the weight of his soul and his dreams, beside me. The time was coming soon to relieve myself of all that weight. But at that moment, sitting beside my good friend with a pitcher of wine between us, and a full clay beaker in my hand, I was in no hurry to stop watching the gentle waters sparkle under our feet.

"'How many of us are left?' I asked the General's batman, as I gazed lazily around at the scattered red shirts in the piazza. Paolo, over with some young women in the afternoon sun, had pulled out his bandoneon, and his lilting melodies were wafting across the stones like laughter.

"'Just these few men you see here,' Aguiar answered. 'Maybe fifty of us. When we left the lake, il Generale dispersed most of the Legion. He sent them away, to find their homes, and wait until the rising begins again. All of them, except these few men.

"'Most of us,' I said, glancing around at the familiar faces, 'were with him in Montevideo.'

"'All of us, il piccolo,' he said, 'We were all but one or maybe two of us on the Speranza.'

"I took a sip of the strong wine, and gazed around the square at faces I knew from that voyage, wondering as I drank about who was missing, who besides Francesco Anzani was absent, as Paolo's dance drifted across the old stones in the failing light of summer's dusk. But I had a warm, full belly for once, and a good friend in Aguiar at my side, and the General was near at hand. So all was well with the world, just then, it was.

"Until I remembered the men on guard, the men below in the darkening valley. And though I was tired and filled with wine and bread, I remembered them. When Umberto and Paolo and I had arrived, no one was eating. And that meant the guards out there had yet to enjoy the good food and the warm hospitality of Morazzone.

"'I must get Umberto,' I said, as I got up on my tired feet again. 'Come with me, Aguiar.'

"'Where are we going?' he said, but I was already several steps out ahead of him, so I don't think he heard me when I answered.

"'We must feed the guard.'

"In a moment I was beside Umberto, and I put my arm around his shoulders. Aguiar strode up from behind us to stand beside the General.

"'Il Generale mio,' I announced, grinning broadly, and then I looked at Umberto. The late summer light in the piazza had taken on that rare golden shade that only comes for a few moments at dusk. The General looked over at me, and I went on, 'Umberto, we must collect some food for the guard, don't you think? Can we get a few baskets, and a bucket of water? And you and I and Aguiar here, we can take it down to them. Non e' vero?'

"'Down to them?' Aguiar said, frowning.

"'Yes, down in the valley below us,' I pointed to where we'd seen the men moving about in the forest above.

"'Il piccolo,' the General said, a dark and weary shadow crossing his blue eyes. With just a nod of his head, he pointed out to us his guards, in their red blouses, standing in pairs eating and drinking at the mouths of the many narrow entrances to the piazza, and then to where the outer guard should be, deeper in the streets. But those men we'd seen on way up the hillside, there were no red shirts among them

"'What did you see?' Aguiar whispered, his eyes staring out of the piazza then toward the edge of town.

"The General was already scanning the forested hilltops across the valley, the tight wrinkles around his eyes cutting deep as he squinted to see into the distance, searching where I had pointed. 'Get everyone out of this piazza. Now,' he barked, and it sent the three of us running.

"So it was, lads, at that very moment, when those Austrian hounds saw the alarm in our movements, they must have seen too Umberto and I pointing down into the vale, and then they saw the scurry of warning in our steps. For at that very instant, I turned and saw Paolo, the singing bandoneon still in his hands and the pretty dark haired neighbor girls gathered around him, at that very moment I saw him fall to the stones like he'd been struck by lightening. Suddenly, there were bugles blaring, and the

151

pretty hum of that little accordion had vanished, silenced under the shouts and cries of the townspeople all around.

"In just one beat of my heart, I swear, I reached Paolo across that stone piazza as everyone around me ran in every direction at once, but, lads, I reached him only in time to see his blood pouring out all over his face. He was gone, O ragazzi, before I could even touch him. An Austrian bullet had taken him straight in the face, breaking his jaw, and knocked off the back of his skull too. He was screaming, amongst all the other screams, but only for an instant. Because he was gone, that quickly, before I reached him across that little piazza."

Burton snapped the bandoneon in his hands shut then with a sharp slap. It was just a little red octagonal box again. The instrument was gone, and so was all the music. "For some reason, I still don't know why, lads, not even now. I guess I loved him, O ragazzi, I guess I loved him. But I took this little bandoneon out of his still warm, his still too soft hands, and then like everyone else in that piazza, I turned and ran back into the narrow streets."

Burton set the little red instrument down in his lap, and carefully, gently, snapped the leather straps down that held it closed. The sound of the leather sliding into place felt like the rattle of stones on a new grave.

"Once I reached the shadows of Morazzone's narrow streets, I stopped and looked back. The piazza was nearly empty of everything but a few overturned carts, a spilled bucket or two next to bread crusts and wine bottles, and the bodies of the dead. Three of them, and among them lying on his back with his head turned and gazing up at the sky, was Paolo. A few short blocks from me, I saw Umberto with his arm around the shoulders of Signor Antonio, who'd taken a bullet in the thigh, and found it hard to walk. Umberto was helping him into the shadows when the hard silence that followed that first volley of Austrian fire fell across the piazza.

"Out in the center, with his fair locks spread on his shoulders and in his red blouse, the General stood with an arm straight out, pointing down into the forest below at the edge of the village. He was shouting out orders in the silence, standing tall and alone on the stones, as if he could not be touched. But his orders told us to retreat our way back into the forest, into the west, from which we'd all come, his orders disappeared then in the blare of Austrian bugles on the hill, sounding the charge.

"Aguiar was nowhere to be seen, but the General stepped toward me. 'Run,' I cried at him, knowing the Austrians were reloading as I called out. But he strode slowly toward me, stepping unevenly on the old stones, as if he had lost his balance, and I realized something was wrong. I thought he'd been hit, somewhere, because it was clearly not the stones, but a limp that halted his labored steps.

"Still, he kept his head high, and he tried to make it seem that he was just walking on without fear. I crouched down and stuffed this bandoneon in my sack, next to the red shirt of Francesco Anzani."

"The red shirt!" cried Robbie, bouncing up onto his knees. "The red shirt!"

But Burton went on as if he hadn't heard my brother's cries. "I tossed the bag over my shoulder, and ran back out to help the General across the square. He put just one hand on my shoulder, said, 'Il Piccolo," but refused more help than that. Somehow, we stepped up our pace, and when the next volley of Austrian fire roared up at us, we were nearly into the dark and out of the bright piazza.

"My eyes searched him up and down, looking for blood or at least a tear in his clothing that would show me where the wound was that could hobble him so. But I could find nothing, not a trace, the only sign of his pain was in the hard set of his teeth, bared in a frown under his mustache. It was, still, a miracle that when that second volley of shot blazed through the piazza, we were both untouched. And somehow, through the grace of a power bigger than all of us, we made it into the shadows of Morazzone's alleys.

"'To the forest! To the west!' the General commanded us, over the calls of the enemy bugles. We knew that their charge was rushing up into the village from the east, and like the General, I saw that our only chance was to get through the valley and then fight them off from the safety of the western hills.

"But the General and I were making poor time, limping on the stones of a winding street, just heading toward where the sun had sunk in the high hills, and an early darkness was falling. It was slow, and it was confusing. I began to fear that the Austrians advance would charge up behind us, and the General and I would be captured long before we could reach the safety of the distant hillside. In my heart I decided that it would be better to die there, on the stones of Morazzone, than to let myself be captured.

"But then from out of a side alley, I heard the shouts of Aguiar's deep voice. 'Generale!' he cried, 'Generale!'

"And I shouted, 'Here, Aguiar! Here!' at the top of my voice. There was a loud clopping echoing around the walls and then out of the shadowy streets emerged black Aguiar leading a saddled black horse.

"'Generale,' he cried, and in moments the batsman had his General mounted. And it was true, the General seemed powerful again on his horse, though it took some help from Aguiar to get him up and mounted. The General's arms were strong, but he had trouble now with his legs, and he needed the batsman's help to lift them to the stirrups. I could see there was no sign of a word or a gesture between them, but I noticed Aguiar acted without orders. Clearly he had seen Il Generale hobbled this way before.

"But like I say, lads, once that old sailor was up on horseback, Il Generale seemed transformed. No longer the old salt stumbling on stones. No. He stood the horse with elegance, and with a shake of his head he tossed his blonde locks back like they were some sort of mane. 'To the forest!' he cried, and then he was off at a dash through the narrow streets of the village."

I asked, "Where were the foreigners?" remembering the bugles Burton told us had already sounded the charge.

"I think they were afraid of us, lad," Burton said, a quizzical grin on his face. "For at that moment, they could have risen upon us and seized us all, every one of us, trapped us right in that square. It should have been a massacre, lads, I tell you, a slaughter. It should have been the end of the Anzani Legion."

"How could he lead you into such a trap?" I asked, and that brought Burton up short. Even now, years and ages later, Jack Burton didn't like doubting the leadership of his General.

"It was indeed, lad, a great mistake," the old man said, his eyes glaring at me now. "Perhaps one of his greatest mistakes, to lead these men into such narrow and confusing straights. But, you know, O ragazzi, I think he too was tired, and hungry, just like Paolo and Umberto and me. And remember, something was wrong; he was not well.

"But even when we were tired and hungry and sick, and even when they had the superior numbers too, and the moment of surprise, even with all of that, my boys, they still feared us. No, lads, I'm wrong. They feared him. They were waiting for dark, and maybe even then they weren't coming at us at all. If it had not been for Umberto and me, pointing down toward them on the hillside, they may never have charged.

"This is the difference, lads, between mercenaries fighting in foreign lands, for money and spoils, and men who fight for their own freedom.

"But on they did come, and Aguiar and I followed the General at a run through the streets and out into the protection of the trees. With the Austrians invading the square behind us, slowly and too cautiously for their own good. Meanwhile, the General tried to gather his Legion in the forests to the west. But everything around us was a great confusion, lads. The General pointed straight at me and Aguiar, and he ordered us, 'Pull them together on that high ground.' He pointed to the foothills across the valley. Then he slid a saber from the scabbard at his side and sliced the air with it. 'You, and you,' he ordered a pair of men, pointing with the tip of the blade. 'Follow me.'

"And with that he turned the horse and dashed back into the streets of Morazzone, with two men in red blouses, bayonets at the ready, right behind him. With just those two men, and a horse, he moved about those alleys and kept the too cautious mercenaries at bay, while darkness fell. I think, perhaps, some of the residents fired a random shot or two, from one window or another, at the invading dogs. But for better than an hour the Austrians were stopped on the other side of the piazza, halted by three men and a horse, moving about in the dark.

"And all the while, Aguiar and I did as we were ordered. We gathered all the Legion up on the top of a tall wooded hill, across the little vale of Morazzone, and we waited in the dark for the Austrian charge."

Burton paused there a moment, and he turned and set the closed bandoneon on the ground, beside the little chest

156

that held his long pipe and that strange tobacco he smoked, with the red shirt folded carefully and laid on top of it. When his hands were free then, he reached over and stroked the great ape on its brow. Zambutti Sam almost cooed at the touch, and his tiny black eyes took Robbie and me in, before they rested again, devotedly, on his master.

"Aguiar and I split up and moved around in the forest, searching for the men of the Legion who'd been scattered or lost, and sending them as we found them up to the high ground the General had chosen. Almost every member of the Anzani Legion knew me from our voyage across the Atlantic, and they all knew, of course, the General's batsman, Aguiar. So it was easy to move through the trees, call them out of hiding, and then send them up to the higher ground where we would make our stand, to await the General's orders.

"It all went smoothly, except for one moment. I was pressing my way along a steep cuff covered in underbrush, when out of the darkness I heard a strange voice call out, 'Il Piccolo.'

"'Who are you?' I answered, wondering whom but the General would call me by that name.

"'Here!' the stranger's voice answered.

"'But who are you?' I called out, and slunk lower to the hillside.

"'It is Antonio,' the voice cried. And then he said, 'I have our friend Umberto,' before his voice broke abruptly.

"I crawled over toward the voice through the brush and found them, in a little clearing beneath the low shadows of a great old hemlock tree. It was Signor Antonio, who knew me only by the name he'd heard the General call me. He was on his knees with blood staining all down one of his legs, and his head was bent, and he was weeping. Beneath him, on the soft brown hemlock bows, many seasons old, Umberto was sprawled. But his legs were splayed awry in a twisted position that told me immediately something was wrong.

"'He's gone, the dear child,' said Signor Antonio, through his tears, once he saw me approaching.

"'What happened?' I asked, as I took those twisted legs of the dead boy and turned them back to a more comfortable position.

"'He was hit in the back,' Signor Antonio said, 'just as we came out of via San Angelo. He was helping me, because of my wound.'

"I nodded my head remembering the two of them leaving the piazza.

"'The Austrians shot him in the back,' Signor Antonio said. 'He fell forward on his face, and from that moment his legs were dead. I dragged him down here, il Piccolo, but this was as far as we got. He died here, with me holding his head, just moments ago. He died right here. Just now.'

"And then old Signor Antonio broke down and wept, as I held Umberto's hand, still warm and still relaxed, just as I'd held poor Paolo's hand not an hour before. In that little stretch of time, just sunset of an August evening in the village of Morazzone, they were both gone, like the day's light. They just came home, and then their lives drained suddenly away, and that was all. Once again, I'd grown close to dear friends, and then, as I always do, I outlived them."

Burton stopped, and I watched as he looked from me to my even younger brother, and a deep sadness I could not understand at my young age flashed across his eyes while he watched my brother Robbie squirming on the rug, beside his little backpack, like the restless child he was. "It is my curse, to out live them all,' Burton whispered, and for once he was not speaking to anyone at all. "And I don't understand why," he whispered. He was silent for just a moment longer, before he went on.

"'So Antonio and I, we carried Umberto back up to the hilltop, where the General had ordered us to gather. There didn't seem anything else to do. And it took us a while, because old Antonio was wounded in the leg from an Austrian bullet. But we climbed the steep hillside with Umberto between us, and then we waited with the others for the Austrian charge, and I guess Umberto became, and Paolo too, true members of those last days of the Anzani Legion.

"We buried him, all of us, quickly, and we laid a big stone over his grave, so he could be found again when all this war was done.

"It wasn't long after that, the General and his pair of legionnaires joined us on the hilltop, and then it was approaching midnight before the foreigners came on, charging down out of Morazzone and then up the dark and wooded hillside at us, and all through that night we repulsed them. Over and over again, from different angles and directions, their white coats came up the hill to no avail. And I'm afraid, O ragazzi, in the tumult of that fight, as they came at us and we retreated or we held our ground or we advanced, back and forth across that steep hillside, somewhere in that tumult, Umberto's plain stone was rolled aside or knocked asunder. Because years later, when I returned to old Morazzone, I found Paolo's grave in the churchyard, not far from signor Antonio's. But though I searched that hillside up and down, and I asked everyone I could find who was of an age to know. No one, none of us, ever found the remains of Umberto Trovesi again. He's gone, lads, every trace of him but what is in my heart has disappeared. All, but what is in my heart."

"We will remember him!" Robbie said, earnestly. And it made Burton grin.

"I suppose you will, ragazzo mio," he said. "Perhaps you will."

But the grin on his face quickly disappeared. "When the dawn of that August morning began to break," he went on, "it was obvious to us all that they still held the little village, and now they were setting fire to the buildings on the outskirts of the town. It became clear we could not hold our forest line against them in the broad daylight, when they could bring their artillery to bear.

"And so, quickly the General gathered the men again, and told us to bear north, using the wooded foothills of the rugged landscape as cover, and using the footpaths in the mountains where the foreign army could not follow. So Aguiar helped the General back onto his horse, and we all retreated quietly and quickly away from Morazzone, heading northward around Varese and into the winding trails above the Valganna.

"I rode with Aguiar on his brown mare, clinging to his shirt as the mare's butt bounced me around. And we followed as close as we could to the General. Again, the foolish Austrians, when they saw us retreating, they did not press after us in a concerted charge that would surely have broken our ranks. No, out of fear, and perhaps out of some rebel respect for the Legion itself, they let us slip out of their grasp.

"But the traveling across that difficult ground, avoiding the roads and easy pathways of the Valganna, was hard. And moving as quickly as we could, with some on foot and some on horseback, even as hard as the General tried, we could not keep the Legion together. There were feints and attacks from the Austrians along the way, and our stragglers fell behind us and into the pursuers' hands. But most of all it was the narrow trails and footpaths we used. The landscape made it impossible for the Austrians to come at us as a whole, for an army of their size could not move through that country in any organized way. But it also meant that we could not keep the Anzani Legion together, moving as we did. Our advance guard became separated from our rear, and some of those in the middle were lost, and stragglers fell behind everywhere along the way.

"We traveled all that day and all of the following night, and in the dawn light the General and Aguiar and I rode out into a clearing in the high hills. Below us, over a short plain we could see Ponte Tresa and the waters of Lago Lugano. It was the Swiss border, and the sight of safety. But as the General looked around him, there were barely twenty of us left. The Anzani Legion was straggled all across the mountains above the Valganna, from here all the way back to Morazzone.

"He turned his horse so he could face the few of us left, and he gave us his last orders. 'Men, you have been true to the dream of Francesco. The dream we all of us shared. But the Anzani Legion is no more.'

"There were shouts of 'No' and 'Never' and 'Viva Anzani,' but the General raised a palm and shook it back and forth. He drew in a deep breath and said, 'In a few moments we will cross that border into safety,' and he pointed out at blue waters of the Lake. 'From there, my friends, we must all go our separate ways, and the Legion must vanish into Switzerland. Vanish from this earth, vanish everywhere but in your hearts.

"'Some of you may stay in Switzerland, and some of you may return quietly into Lombardia, or head back to Genova. Some of you may hide with the French.' He said this because, as all of us knew who'd sailed on the Speranza, he was thinking of his Anita and his children in Nice.

"'But wherever you go, you must keep your ear to the ground. Keep your bayonet at hand, and listen for the hoof beats to rise again, and rise again we will, my comrades.

161

For we are beaten now, but we are not vanquished. In our hearts we keep the spirit of Francesco Anzani alive.'

"And so it was, we rode down onto Ponte Tresa and crossed quietly over into Switzerland, and we each went our many ways, to escape, and to await the General's call."

"But what about the red shirt?" Robbie protested.

"Yeah," I added my two bits worth, feeling cheated to have come so far without an end.

Jack Burton smiled, and he gazed over at his shirt on that chest. I thought then he was admiring it, remembering its story. But as the years have passed, I think now that Burton was pondering whether he needed another long draught from that strange pipe inside the chest in order to complete his tale. But the end was close at hand now, and so he charged ahead.

"Once we'd crossed the border and we were safe, Aguiar pulled his horse up, and he whispered quietly to me, 'Stay with him, Burtoni, and I'll go on ahead.' And at that he slipped me down from the back of his brown mare, and looked over at our General.

"'I'll ride ahead, sir, and find us a place,' he announced.

"The General, who seemed distracted, just nodded his head. Aguiar, with a kick of his heels, was off galloping to the north along the lakeshore toward Lugano. I walked alongside the General's horse for a while, as we wandered along behind Aguiar, and then the General seemed to come around, as if he'd been roused from a dream.

"'Il Piccolo,' he said to me, stretching out an arm, 'Com up here, behind me.' And he took his boot out of the stirrup so I could use it to mount the horse.

"With a hoist and a lift I was up and seated behind him on the black horse, and as I settled in, I noticed for the first time the streams of sweat that had run down from under his hat brim and dampened his beard. He was flushed red too and his eyes, now that I was close to him I saw, they were dark and shaded.

"'Let's go,' he said. 'Andiamo, mi' piccolo.'

"And with the horse at a leisurely canter, we followed northward after Aguiar. It was as if now that we had crossed into Switzerland, now that we had left the dream, his dream and Anzani's dream, left it all behind, in the burning alleys of Morazzone, now all of his weariness could come to rest upon him at once.

"And rest it did, lads, because it was not long, a half an hour or so, before the General nearly collapsed and fell from the horse. Now I understood what his batsman was up to, for he knew the General had come to the end of his tether. Aguiar had left me to get his General to the city, but I knew without asking where we were headed. Where ever we could find him a bed, a place to recuperate. This was where Aguiar had gone. To find a hospice for his leader.

"At that moment, as I held him in the saddle and we cantered along, I thought it would be my fate to watch him die too. Anzani, Paolo and Umberto, and all their dreams, and now Il Generale, too.

"But I stiffened my arms and grasped the saddle horn, and I held him up and kicked that horse into a lope. It was the best that I could do, without losing my hold on him and letting him fall to the ground,

"Aguiar was waiting for us, on the road at the outskirts of Lugano, and he led us to an inn by the lake and we took him down from the horse and carried him inside.

He was barely conscious, but as he came down from the back of that horse into our arms, he grumbled and moaned at the bending of his knees and anytime we moved his legs. This man who had run and fought and ridden across Lombardia and the Piedmonte, who'd spent hours and hours, if not days, on his feet marching forward, without ever a complaint, with always a grin or a snarl on his face, and a strong word to urge the rest of us on, here he whimpered and moaned at being lifted from his horse, and just bending a knee.

"When we had him down, he looked up at me out of his fever and exhaustion, and he said, 'Il Piccolo,' in recognition. Then he was gone into pain and delirium again.

"The inn Aguiar had found was run by Swiss who had their eyes on the border, and knew who Il Generale was. So they gave him a little room at the rear of the inn with a bed and a chair, and out the window a view of the ice blue lake and the alpine peaks around it.

"And through that first night, as Aguiar and I took turns sitting up with him, I did not believe the General would survive. I was certain he would die before the light of another day. And so I resolved that, somehow, I needed to give him Ciccio's shirt, before he was gone. He needed to know of Francesco's undying faith in him, even though they had disagreed so fiercely before my Ciccio was gone.

"So I went to my pack and pulled out caro Ciccio's red shirt from where I'd tucked it under Paolo's too silent bandoneon. And as I took it out, I promised myself that for the memory of Umberto and Paolo, I would learn to play that little instrument. I would learn to make it sing, as Paolo had. That would keep something of them alive, as long as I was around." Burton paused, and again his eyes seemed dazed. "As long as I'm around," he repeated.

Then he went straight on with his story. "I held Ciccio's shirt in my lap, waiting and hoping against hope for a moment of clarity in the General's long night. Just one chance, before he too departed from these earthly shores, and sailed off to that other, further foreign land.

"It was in the blackest part of that August night, turning toward the autumn of September, that the General moved his legs in his sleep, and the very pain of them roused him from his deep sleep. With a grimace and a moan, he looked up at me from the pillows, and his dark, shaded eyes seemed confused and lost. I feared he would just plunge back into his delusion, not knowing where he was. But as his eyes lingered on me, he began to smile with recognition. 'Il Piccolo,' he said, as if seeing me there reminded him of where he was, and what causes and struggles we were about. 'Piccolo,' he said again, and he was ready to fall back to his rest.

"'Il Generale,' I said, lest he slip away, 'Il Generale, I have something for you.' And as I said it, I realized how much this scene was like that night when my Zio Francesco had given me this very shirt, and with it the task to deliver it. 'I have something for you,' I repeated. 'It's from Francesco.'

"'Francesco,' he said, confused again for a moment in his illness.

"'Zio Ciccio nostro,' I said.

"His eyes brightened and a little smile grew faintly across his lips. He nodded his head and said, in a whisper, 'Anzani.'

"'My General, on the night my Zio died, he gave this to me,' and I held out the red shirt toward him in the bed. 'He told me that this was my most important task. Ciccio said there would come a time when you would feel betrayed, and all would seem lost. And that I must, above all, give this to you when those defeats rained down upon you.'

"And then I laid the folded red blouse on the General's chest, feeling a deep pride at having at long last fulfilled those final orders from my dying Zio.

"The General seemed confused at first, and he put his hands on the red blouse. His eyes, so dark and dim, gazed at it and he asked, without looking away from the shirt, 'This is not mine?'

"'No, my General,' I said. 'That is our Ciccio's shirt. He ordered me to bring it to you.'

"The General lay there, with both hands resting on that red shirt, and I suppose, lads, he felt in that plain red cloth all the battles across South America it had seen, and all the dangers it had shared with him, at his side, and survived. I don't really know what he felt, my little ragazzi, but I can tell you that his eyes filled with tears, and they ran down his cheeks like the sweat I'd seen on him the day before. 'Francesco,' he said. His old and loyal friend, lads.

"Just then a bird sang in the night, and he raised a hand from the red blouse on his chest, and he said, 'Listen!' I turned and looked out the open window toward the lake, and saw the soft moonlight on its waters.

"'A nightingale?' I said to him, not sure of what I heard.

"But he didn't answer, and in just that moment, I looked back at him, and he was asleep again, or passed down under the fever and exhaustion he suffered."

"Did he die?" Robbie asked, interrupting again.

"No, lad," Burton whispered with a warm smile. "Not that night anyway."

Jack Burton drew in a deep breath, and then he gazed for a moment at me and then at Robbie, and finally he said, "Every three or four hours the Swiss brought soup to him. That first night it was just broth, and then as the days went by, the soups grew thicker and hardier and after a while they came with a crust of bread. And never once, unless it was

Aguiar who took care of it on the sly, though I don't know how, never once did I see any money change hands. Those innkeepers never asked for a cent, only for the chance to help bring our General back to life. And slowly, with our care and their good food, he did come back to life."

"What was wrong with him?" I asked.

"Oh, lad, he had in his legs and hips a hard rheumatism, and all the rest of his life, when he tired himself beyond some great extreme, and even when the weather turned, it could cripple him like this.

"Aguiar knew it, and he told me so himself. I think, though the General would never admit to this on his own, I think he suffered that pain all the time, sempre, lads, sempre. But only when he was exhausted or sick did he ever let it show. The rest of the time, in front of us, his men, you would never know he was anything but fit and strong.

"It was a few days later, when he was much stronger, that I came in to relieve Aguiar and take my turn sitting with the General, and Aguiar stood up and walked to the doorway, but he didn't leave the room. The General was now sitting up in bed, and he reached over and patted the seat of a chair next to the bed. 'Il piccolo,' he said, 'sit down here, my young friend.'

"Aguiar stopped and leaned on the doorknob as if he was waiting for something. A grin spread across his face, and the General went on, 'My good batsman here, he has told me all about your journey, trying to catch up with the Legion. Walking all that way, and finding along the way those two good lads who saved us in Morazzone, and then we left their bones to rest there. He told me all about it, il piccolo. Quite an adventure you've had, little one.'

"I looked over at Aguiar, and he was still grinning like he'd swallowed the last drop of brandy in the last bottle on board. It was true, I'd told him over these last few days in Lugano, waiting for the General to come around, my whole story of starting out alone and then finding Umberto and Paolo. But I wasn't ever planning for him to pass my story on. It was just talk to pass the long nights of watching over il Generale.

"With a nod of his head toward his batsman, the General said, 'Aguiar.' His voice carried that natural authority of an order again, returning to him with his strength hour by hour. The black man needed no more than that to know what was demanded of him. From out of somewhere in the General's gear he retrieved the red shirt and handed it over to il Generale. I thought Aguiar might start to laugh out loud, his grin was so broad. And then came one of the very greatest moments in all my days, ragazzi, maybe even the greatest moment of all.

"'Il piccolo,' the General said, 'you have served us well on this campaign. By delivering this to me, in that my darkest hour, you have fulfilled our dear Ciccio's command, and it has given to me the memory of Francesco's undying heart and eternal faith. As he knew it would, it has restored in me the dream to press on, until my dying breath if need be, to reach our dream.'

"'But now,' the General didn't pause. 'This red shirt has done its task. I do not need it anymore, mio piccolo, for what it means remains in my heart. And so, my young friend, I give it now to you. I am as sure as I can be that Francesco would want you to have it, for you have earned it, il piccolo.' And then he passed on to me that red shirt of Francesco Anzani, folded into my hands. As I took it from him, he said, 'il piccolo rosso.'

"It was good soldier Aguiar, across the room, who laughed out loud finally, and then he gave me my name, lads. 'Il Rosso,' Aguiar said with a shout.

"'Il Rosso,' the General repeated with a curt nod of his head. The 'piccolo' was gone."

"Il Rosso," Robbie said.

"Il Rosso," I said.

And then we all laughed together.

"So that, little ragazzi, is how I came by my name. "

"Il Rosso," Robbie repeated, with a hush of reverence in his tone. My little brother's eyes were glowing with excitement. I suppose when Jack Burton had looked at mine, he thought the same thing.

"So where did you go then?" I asked Jack Burton. "When the General got better? The three of you? Where did you go next?"

"Yeah," Robbie said, his head snapping back and forth from me to Burton. "The General and you and Aguiar. You three!" He didn't need to add, 'just like us!'

"No, no, lads," Burton said. "It's getting late and it's time to turn in." Then the old man drew in a monstrous big breath and yawned like an old lion in the afternoon son. "It's time for you lads to head home."

That drew us both up short. "But," I said.

"We're coming with you," Robbie protested. "Just like Aguiar and the General."

"Like Paolo and Umberto," I said.

"O ragazzi," Burton said, giving us both a stern look. "Stop your dreaming, and think, my little ragazzi."

There was a moment's pause, and then Robbie stood up. "We're coming with you," he announced. "I've thought about it."

I guess the remarkable thing is that Jack Burton didn't laugh at us then. His face stayed as stern and serious as the dawn before a battle.

"But, laddies," he said, "think about the plan. I've got a show to do tomorrow night, and the feeding of Jessie the elephant tomorrow afternoon."

"The what?" I said.

"You boys come here tomorrow afternoon, and you'll see. But if you try to hide from your parents for a whole day, why," he shook his head back and forth, worried, "why they'll have the police all over us and, then . . . "

"We'll get caught!" Robbie said, but he pitched his little shoulders back anyway.

"That's right, mi' ragazzo. So you go on home tonight, and you boys sleep in your beds, and never let on to anyone that we talked at all. That you were even here tonight.

"And then tomorrow, at highest noon, meet me here by the big tent, and we'll make our final plans." He leaned forward in his chair, and slowly he glared at Robbie and then at me. His blazing eyes bored through us, and I have to admit, he frightened me. I suppose that was his intention. "Tomorrow. High noon. The Big Top." He pointed a finger at Robbie. "We'll make our plans." Then he pointed it at me. "Now, go." He sank back in his chair. "Go on home, miei ragazzi."

And so Robbie and I trudged back to our house, and crept through that window and crawled back into our beds. But it was a long time that night before we fell asleep. And Robbie kept that knapsack of his packed, and stuffed under his bed, even though it raised one leg off the floor and made the bed wobble when he moved in it. Still, he fell asleep before I did, and in his sleep I heard him say, "Il Rosso."

*　　　　*　　　　*

170

At a quarter to noon we were at the door to the Big Top, but so was half our little town. Every kid we knew was there, and a goodly number of adults from town, too. The crowd milled around, kicking at the sand and chatting, and a game of rough and tumble tag had started up around behind the tent.

Jack Burton was nowhere to be seen, so Robbie and I went round to his red Buick, but he wasn't there either. As we poked around at his tent, hoping to find him away from the crowd, we heard a loud snort from the white cart.

"Sammy is in there," I said, and at that Robbie and I went over to the little window where this whole adventure started. But this time there was no need for me to boost my brother up in the air to look in.

"Zambutti Sam!" Robbie called out, his little arms akimbo and his sneakers spread out solid and set in the grass.

We heard a little cough of recognition, and then the gorilla's black face rose up into the barred window.

"Sammy," we shouted.

His small, black eyes were soft and watery, and he gave us a gentle little moan for a hello. It seemed a shame that he was locked up inside there, but I think we both understood that Burton had to keep up the appearance of the wild gorilla for his show, and that an ape like that, strolling around loose in our little town was surely not safe. At worst, someone was likely to take a shot at Sammy out of fear. At best, some policeman or warden would haul Zambutti Sam away to a zoo, and he'd be lost to Jack Burton forever, and to us too. So we understood why Sammy sat inside his cage during the days. It was all an illusion, just like the way we'd crept back to out beds the night before.

Still I wandered around to the door at the back, and found a little padlock hanging from the latch. But with just a turn of the wrist it fell open, not even locked, just set to look like it was. Robbie and I creaked open the wooden door, framed in steel, and then Sammy came forward to us.

Inside he had his short, curved stool, and the rug that had been the floor to the tent last night, the rug Robbie and I had stretched out on to listen to Burton. It was spread out now over part of the ape's small cage. Part of it was rolled up against the wall. And the little chest was there, tucked carefully beside the stool.

The little room inside the trailer was dark and warm, but it was comfortable. And I noticed for the first time how Burton had pulled the Buick around so Sammy's cart was tucked under one of the big low oaks, so it would be all through the afternoon under a cool heavy shade.

Sammy sat at the edge of the door on his haunches, so that Robbie and then I could stroke his hairy graying brow, just the way we'd seen Burton do the night before. And I noticed then how old the ape seemed, with streaks of gray and white across his head and over his shoulders.

That was when we heard a cheer rise up, and in the midst of it Burton's deep voice calling out, "Avanti!"

It took us only a moment to say goodbye to Zambutti Sam for now, and softly close the door to his cart. I know we didn't think to latch it again, and I'm sure we left that little open padlock lying on the ground. But we heard again Burton calling out, "Andiamo, Jessica, andiamo!" and another cheer went up from the children's voices. And with a dash across the schoolyard, we were back beside the Big Top.

*   *   *

It was quite a sight to see, at least in our little town. Here came the Indian elephant, stepping gingerly and slowly across our schoolyard. And beside her Burton rolled himself along across the grass, one hand on his wheelchair, and in the other he carried a short thick stick with a blunt iron hook on its hand. And ranging around behind the animal all the kids in town, curious enough to get close, but with every step of the elephant, like a nervous swarm of bees, they were slipping and shifting and scurrying off to the side and away.

"Avanti," Burton shouted, "avanti!" And the elephant moved ponderously down the gradual slope of the schoolyard and out onto the paved street. From there, it was easier for Burton to maneuver his chair alongside the animal.

There was another carnie, a young guy in a denim shirt and an open leather vest, who moved along behind the elephant, helping Burton lead her down the street. He carried a short stick too. But he never said a word, and he tried to seem invisible, just part of the swarms of kids. It was clear to me that Jack Burton was part of the show. The spectacle of watching an old man in a wheelchair lead an elephant down the street was clearly part of this display.

The whole deal was advertising for the evening show, of course. A little taste for free of the wonders to be seen beneath the Big Top that very evening, to all who'd pay the fare. And so down the street through our town went Jessica the Indian elephant, with Jack Burton in his wheelchair leading her along.

They came to my father's gas station, and there stood my father beside a big steel washtub, with the gray-green garden hose in his hand. And as we approached, in the lieu of the elephant, Burton rolled himself up, and shook our father's hand. And they both grinned and, I suppose they knew it was good for everybody's business, because they spoke to one another happily, and Robbie and I lay low, off to the side. We were afraid, you see, that if Jack Burton knew that his new chum here was our Pop, that would be the end of our great escape with the circus. So we hung back and hid around the corner of the gas station where the empty pop bottles were stacked in wooden cases. But we couldn't go away entirely.

See, our father was about to water Jessica the elephant. He stood there, in his gas station uniform with its shirt all oil-stained, but with a straw fedora cocked on his head because he knew the photographer from the weekly paper would be there. And he wanted to look good. That straw fedora sported a silk band that was striped cream and dark burgundy. He was not wearing his gas company cap, not this day.

And then, as Jack Burton maneuvered the animal up toward the steel tank, my Pop looked up and his eyes wandered across the swarm of kids, his eyes squinting under the August sun. We knew, instantly, that he was looking for us. He wanted his two boys in that shot on the front page of the weekly, beside the great gray elephant. I grabbed Robbie and dragged him back behind the station, out of sight.

"Hey, I want to see it," Robbie whined.

"We can't let Mr. Burton find out that's our Dad," I said.

Robbie understood the problem immediately. His face settled into a worried scowl, and he looked back up the hill toward the motel where Burton had been thrown out by ol' Mrs. Coogan and where the hoochie-coochie girls were probably still resting on their beds, waiting for some little boy to come by, and then he looked the other way toward

Main Street. His nose scrunched up like he smelled something.

"Follow me," he said then, and ran around to the back of the garage, far from the pumps and the watering elephant.

In a moment, I was following him as we climbed up a pair of used tractor tires tilted against the wall, onto a fuel oil tank and then with a shimmy and a leap we pulled ourselves up onto the flat tarred roof of the station. It was warm enough under that August sun that the tar was soft, but not hot enough to be sticky. We ran across it and in a moment we were looking out over the brick ledge at the front of the gas station. Though the roof stank a little of the softened tar, we didn't care, because we were staring down from the big 's' in 'Standard Oil' onto the amazing show below.

There my father had the hose in hand, and Jessica the elephant had her trunk in the tank. She was sucking up a trunk full of water, and then shooting it happily into her mouth. Pop thought he'd be funny, I guess, because he lifted the stream of water from his hose up onto the elephant's back. She let loose a trumpet of delight at that cool water, and all the kids down below us moved back two steps in unison, it seemed. Father was laughing, and he had a big grin on his face, and he used his thumb to jet the water up onto the elephant's dusty, leathery back.

Burton and his carnie friend were looking around, a little nervously at all the kids, I guess because they knew Jessica the elephant better than the rest of us. But our Pop was having himself a time, and I think we were pretty proud of him, right then. It made me wonder why Robbie was so full of running away. This was pretty exciting, and we could still go home at night, you see.

It was getting pretty warm on top of that tar roof, so Robbie laid down on his stomach on the brick ledge, and he lifted his feet up off the black tar. It looked pretty damn cool, and I was thinking about doing the same thing myself, because my feet were getting warm, too.

But right then Jessica the elephant leaned forward and pulled her trunk out of the steel watering tank. Her trunk was, by God, all full and loaded. And she pointed it straight out at my father's chest, as he was laughing and spraying her with water, and with the blast of a bass trombone, she let loose with a whole trunk full of water that hit our Pop on the chest and sat him down onto the seat of his pants right on the concrete driveway. He was drenching wet with water and elephant snot, sitting on his duff in the driveway, that hose still in his hand piping water up in the air like a fountain. And that snazzy straw fedora of his was floating along across the concrete toward Main Street, riding on the run off of oil and elephant snot.

And everyone was laughing. The kids all around, Burton and his carnie pal, and our Pop too, sitting in the puddle under his own fountain. And of course, Robbie and I were laughing too.

Then what happened next, because it all happened at once, happened fast. Robbie was bouncing on his stomach from his laughter, and suddenly he started to slip off the roof. He was going head first, so I grabbed his belt to hang onto him. His arms were flailing out in the air, and he dragged a shower of gravel off the roof ledge, it rattled loudly off the 'S' and then a piece of the bright red letter broke loose and tumbled down toward the concrete driveway below. My feet rose up off the tar roof, and Robbie's weight started to pull me over too, but instinctively, I set my sneakers against that inside wall of the ledge and I fell backwards, back toward the roof. Meanwhile, that heavy red glass from the 's' hit the concrete and shattered with a loud crystalline jangle, and I think I screamed. But somehow, I had gotten Robbie righted and back up balanced on the ledge.

That was when our mother stepped out of the doorway of the station, onto the shattered red letter on the concrete. She looked up and Robbie's eyes met hers. Then her mouth dropped open. I know she yelled out our names, though I don't remember hearing it. I stood up beside my brother and looked down at half of the town looking up at us. But I don't recall the look on Mother's face, or on Pop's. What I saw was Jack Burton, a crooked grin spread all across his lips, and I swear, he winked at me. Or at us. Because then Robbie shoved himself back onto his feet on the tar roof, and he said plainly, calmly to me, "We better get down from here."

He turned crisply and crossed the roof at a run. It took just a leap and a bounce on those old tractor tires, and we were back on solid ground. And on the run again.

At supper that night Robbie and I were expecting the third degree. After nearly falling off the station roof, and breaking that big red sign, we were both sure it meant going to bed early, being grounded for many long, boring summer days, with no deserts for the foreseeable future, if ever again. It was enough to cement our resolve to run away. But what was worst of all, we both knew it was now going to be harder than ever to break out and get to the circus to meet up with Jack Burton. And we feared our dreams of that fine escape were dying fast and sure.

But at the table, though my Mother frowned a lot, Pops was having none of it. He was still full of his adventure with Jessica the Indian elephant, and so he laughed a lot, and talked about it, telling the story over and over of how it felt to have an elephant hit him with a jet of water. Patting his chest and retailing again with joy how that powerful stream of water and elephant juice had sat him on his tail, he even included Robbie's close call, and the crashing letter 's' in his yarn, as it all grew bigger and funnier the longer and more often he told it. The more he laughed about it all, the more my Mother frowned.

And to top it all off, he leaned forward at one point and pulled out of his pocket a handful of tickets. Fanned out in his hand were four tickets to the circus that very night. "That fellow in the chair," Pops said, 'That circus fellow. Burton. He gave me a pair of these."

"And where did the other two come from?" Mother said, showing no emotion. Which of course, meant the worst.

Pops just smiled, and tried not to look too guilty.

"I'm not going," said Mother.

I glanced furtively over at Robbie, and saw that both our flagging hopes were rising again.

"Oh, come on, Melody," pleaded my Father

It went back and forth like that a couple more times, and then my Mother simply stood up from the table, and without so much as a word, left the room. I was carefully quiet. Robbie wasn't as good.

"Can we go, Dad?" he begged.

My father handed us a couple of the tickets and said, "You boys run ahead. Your Mother," he looked out the doorway of the kitchen where we ate, "and I will catch up with you."

Then he stood, still gazing out the door my Mother had stepped through. And he said. "But be good kids, and clear the table first, do the dishes, before you go. Right?"

I nodded yes, clutching my ticket tightly in my hand.

"You bet," Robbie sang out, way too loudly.

Father left as I was poking Robbie, and telling him to hold it down.

Robbie had his knapsack stuck under the bench seat beneath him, when Jack Burton, dressed in his intense red blouse and with a flat black beret cocked on his head, rolled himself into the single ring of the Big Top. "Maestro Il Rosso," his grandest voice boomed out to the house, "presents to you now, this very evening, the horrifying man-beast from deep in the jungles of highest Zambutti."

And then Shirley and Red, the two hoochie-coochie girls, came striding out into the ring, each of them pulling a red velvet rope, and they were dressed in these green and white sequined swimsuits, I'd call them. The men in the crowd let loose with a wave of whistles and hoots that died very quickly, on the pointed elbows of their wives. Shirley's and Red's faces were all painted up too, and on their heads, braided into the big buns of hair, stood little sequined princess crowns that each sported a tall frilly feather. Shirley's was white, and Red's was green. And of course, they were wearing spiked high heels, sparkling with the same sequins.

Attached to the other end of their red velvet ropes was a stall steel cage, maybe ten feet square and six foot tall. It was draped with a red curtain. This cage, while it was imposing and black, still looked like it was wired together with bailing twine, and it shivered as it rolled across the dirt in the ring.

"Thank you, my lovelies, thank you," boomed Jack Burton, as Shirley and Red laid their ropes on the ground and then retreated to stand just outside the rear corners of the cage. Burton rolled himself around beside the cage, and began to sing out the dangers of "Darkest Africa" and its "deep impenetrable jungles" covering the "long forbidden islands" where he had been lost for years, and where finally he himself had captured "Zambutti Sam, the wild man-beast."

At that, the cage shivered again, and hearing the sound of his name, the mountain gorilla let loose a low, sinister growl. Then as Shirley and Red tugged at something, the red curtain dropped to the ground to reveal Sammy. He bolted from one end of the cage to the other, on all fours, charging toward the crowd and making the people jump in their seats. When he charged toward where Robbie and I sat, I noticed he was wearing make-up, streaks of bright, blood red underneath his eyes and at the corners of his mouth. Whenever he charged toward Shirley or Red, at the corners of the cage, they would scream loud and shrill, and jump away from the bars as if their lives were at risk. After he'd frightened every section of the bleachers, Zambutti Sam retreated back to the rear of the cage, and sat glaring around at us all for a while, as if he was choosing his victim. Once the crowd was quiet and everyone thought Zambutti Sam had settled down, the gorilla rose up on his hind legs for the first time, and then bellowed out some kind of awful rebel yell that he had to have been taught, for it sounded like no human utterance and surely no ape had ever screamed so. And then he beat his chest like a drum. His head lolled back and forth on his neck, and the horrible yell sank down into a vicious snarl, and then the sound of it frightened even me, though only a few hours ago Robbie and I had been stroking Sammy's gray, weathered brow.

Burton rolled himself over to the cage then, and in his hand he unfurled on the ground now a long leather whip. He gave it a snap, and at that sound, Sammy landed again on all fours and charged around and around the cage. Shirley and Red stepped back, as if in fear that this King Kong might drag then into his imprisoned grasp. But Burton cracked the whip on the ground again, and called out, "Zambutti," and now the ape fled back to a far corner of his cage. Then Shirley and Red together opened a door into the pen, and in rolled Burton, the whip coiled in his hand.

It was quite a show from there, as Jack Burton cracked and snapped the whip, and seemed to force the wild beast through a series of puppy dog tricks. Sammy rolled over, he stood on one leg on top of a barrel, he walked on his hands. And of course, there were somersaults and leaps. And at the end, for the finale, Burton was sitting in his chair, both arms in the air, at the front of the cage, begging for applause from the crowd. But Sammy behind him was creeping forward, his ivory fangs bared with some sort of red greasy drool dripping from his mouth, until at precisely the moment when the ape's paws were nearly on him, and the crowd had fallen into a fearsome silence, Red and Shirley together let loose with a timed and terrified pair of screams. At that moment, Burton twisted, and turned his wheelchair to the side, twirling it up onto just one wheel for a moment. And the ape went somersaulting across the dirt floor right where the old man's wheelchair had been, while Burton rolled himself agilely out of the ape's grasp and then out of the cage, as the two hoochie-coochie beauties opened the gate for him and slammed it behind his chair, amidst peals of delighted laughter from the crowd.

And so, as Sammy charged around the cage in melodramatic anger, Burton took his bows, almost rising out of his chair, and the two girls raised the red curtain up again. Strutting like TV bathing beauties on the runway, they picked up the red velvet ropes and pulled the snarling Sammy away, hidden behind the curtain, locked in his cage.

In a moment, Burton was gone, and a sad hobo clown was sweeping up the dirt floor where Sammy's cage had been. The clown chased a brown clog of dirt the size of a hotdog around the ring. He'd step near it, and then wrinkle his nose up into an amazing prune face for the crowd. It had to be a stinking chunk that poor Zambutti Sam had left behind. Or so they would have us believe.

How Robbie and I laughed and laughed at the clown, and his little stinking mess. Wherever he swept it, it hopped like a bug away from him. A couple of times, it popped up in the air. Once it seemed to be headed flying straight into the crowd, and everyone was laughing, pushing and shoving to get out of its way. Finally the silent clown tossed a bucket of water at the clever little heap of dung, and that seemed to dampen its wings.

So he pulled out a giant purple dustpan out of his baggy pants, and held just a tiny little paint brush in his other hand. With a proud nod to the crowd, and a fresh cock of his broken hat, he turned and stooped as he strode toward the mess, at last to do his job and clean it up. But then, at the very last minute, his poor feet in those oversize shoes slipped one way, and though for a moment he caught his balance, the wet mud flew, and still his feet when out from under him in a crazy ballet. So he danced this way and that until, at last, he belly-flopped down onto the ground and right on top of Zambutti Sam's little mess. Robbie and I laughed so hard that little brother nearly slipped off the bench and fell down though the bleachers.

When the clown stood up, a huge red frown on his white face, the whole front of him was muddy brown, or worse. His nose wrinkled up in that big brown prune face again, and as he looked forlornly up at us, the lights went down and we were all plunged into the blackest darkness.

It was only a moment before the lights came back up, but our clown was gone. The ring was empty, and a blare of trumpets announced the entrance of Jessica the elephant. The carnie in the leather vest was there, leading her into the ring, but he was in a royal blue tuxedo now. "Ladies and Gentlemen, Signori e Signore, enter the massive pachyderm," he announced over the sounding horns. And up on Jessica's back rode Shirley and Red, still in their little red and green swimsuits, except now their midriffs were bare, and in their naked navels sparkled something I was sure were diamonds. Jessica stepped slowly into the ring, and the two girls leapt from its back onto the ground on either side of the elephant. And Shirley and Red, with their tops jiggling as if they might come loose, my eyes couldn't decide which one of those diamond navels to watch.

But at that instant, Robbie poked me in the ribs. "What?" I complained, but I said no more.

Robbie pointed down to the main entrance of the tent, and there were Father and Mother. He was sporting his straw fedora again, though it was a bit stained and dusty from the afternoon, and she was wearing a black frown. Pop was looking this way and that in the crowd, searching for us.

"Let's go find Mr. Burton," Robbie whispered, as he slouched down and put his two hands on his little pack.

I wasn't so sure I wanted to miss more of the show, what with Shirley and Red losing clothing with each succeeding act, but I was still game for the fun. So Robbie and I slipped down through the risers, and crawled beneath them and out under the canvas wall of the big tent. I knew then, as I remember it now, I wasn't so determined to run away as Robbie was, but I did come along with him. Maybe it was to keep him safe. Maybe just to see what would happen. All I had was a spare pair of Connies and a summer jacket in my bag, and I hadn't loaded up any of my valuables the way Robbie had. In that khaki green pack of his, he had his four favorite toy soldiers, and a red toy motorcycle, and his little telescope for peering at the stars. But I hadn't even brought my Bob Gibson baseball card, so I guess I have to admit I wasn't really planning on going anywhere. I was just along for the ride.

So, with one last glance back through the bleachers at the diamond navels of Shirley and Red, I crawled out under the canvas. Robbie was already up and gone by the time I stood up outside the Big Top. I looked both ways, but there was no sign of my little brother. So at a walk, rather than a run, I headed for where I knew he had gone.

He was standing under that oak tree, the backpack strapped tight on his back, his feet planted square on the ground, but his head was cast down in dejection. The great red Buick, with the white convertible top, was gone. And so was the white cart, the cage of Zambutti Sam, with its exotic legend on the side: 'Far from the Cape of Lost Hope.' There was nothing but tire tracks and disappointments waiting for us under that oak tree. Jack Burton was gone.

*   *   *

And so, that night Robbie began his search for Jack Burton, Il Rosso, the search that would come to preoccupy both of us from that day to this. That night we wandered all through the town, asking everyone we knew. But most of our little hometown was under the Big Top, ogling at Shirley and Red, amazed at the big circus elephant. They only remembered the way Burton turned his chair on one wheel and escaped the grasp of the wild beast. They knew nothing of his other escape.

"Just another carnie," everyone said when we asked. "They are always here and gone." They said, "Just like a carnie." And the more often than not, they would ask, "Did he steal something from you?"

Perhaps he did. Perhaps he stole our dreams. I know he stole our hearts.

One night about a week later my Father came home from the station for his supper with a story to tell.. He said he was talking with a highway patrolman who'd stopped for a Coke and some peanuts at the station. "This patrolman told me he saw a red Buick, just like that Burton fellow's, speeding along in the night a week or so ago."

Robbie and I held our breath, I'm afraid, trying not to let on. Father had a little glint in his eye as he went on with his yarn. "This patrolman, he swears as that car rolled past him, he saw the monkey driving it. So he flipped on his lights and gave chase, but that big Buick eight just stepped on out, and it was long gone across the state line."

There was a moment of dead quiet, and then my Mother started to laugh. "Artie," she said, "don't be teasing the boys."

*　　　*　　　*

It wasn't until a few years had passed, and I'd studied some history in high school, that I realized we'd truly been had. I went to my little brother, who was still down in the middle grades, and told him it was all a pack of lies.

"It has to be, Robbie," I said. "Add it up. If he was really on the Speranza, then that means he was better than a hundred and twenty years old. Right when we were talking to him."

Robbie nodded yes, but I could tell in some deep part of his heart, it didn't matter. He still believed in Il Rosso. "I know," Robbie said. "It can't be."

"He was lying to us," I said.

But it was a good lie. Because even now, wherever Robbie lands in this big wide world, my brother always lingers awhile. He always looks around for signs of that strange man, and he asks after Jack Burton. Everywhere he goes. He's still in search of the last slight trace of Il Rosso.

And I know now, of course, as does my little brother who searches for Jack Burton still, there is no such thing in the world as an Island Gorilla. Nor is there any place in all the continent of Africa and all her surrounding islands that is called Zambutti. But there was a Zambutti Sam, I swear. I saw the beast with my own eyes and I believed in him, just as my brother did.

There was Zambutti Sam. We saw him.

*   *   *

And so to this day whenever my brother finds something, a scrap of paper, an old circus poster, an old timer's story about an amazing ape, word of it comes straight away to me, always directly to me. Because Robbie knows only I will understand, only I will never laugh at him, only I will respond as quickly as I can, when the word reaches me of some lost trace on the trail of Burton of the Red Shirt.

ALSO BY SANDRO DARIOSTO

THE LAST GOOD RUN

BURTON THE RED:
An omnibus edition containing the first three adventures of
Jack Burton
including

BURTON WITH THE THOUSAND

BEYOND ASPROMONTE

Forthcoming from per sempre Anita Edizione:

HANDS OF THE BIRD AND OTHER STORIES

THE WISDOM RUN